The Adventures of
Ralphy

and the
Awesome
Trio

Linda D. Vagnetti
Illustrated by Erin Abramowicz

The Adventures
of
Ralphy
and the Awesome Trio

Linda D. Vagnetti

Illustrations by Erin Abramowicz

ZIMBELL HOUSE
PUBLISHING
UNION LAKE, MICHIGAN

For permission requests, write to the publisher at the address below:
"Attention: Permissions Coordinator"
Zimbell House Publishing, LLC
PO Box 1172
Union Lake, Michigan 48387
mail to: info@zimbellhousepublishing.com

© 2017 Linda D. Vagnetti
© 2017 Illustrations by Erin Abramowicz
Book and Cover Design by The Book Planners
A Division of Zimbell House Publishing
http://www.TheBookPlanners.com

Published in the United States by Zimbell House Publishing
http://www.ZimbellHousePublishing.com
All Rights Reserved

Print ISBN: 978-1-945967-65-8
Kindle ISBN: 978-1-945967-66-5
Digital ISBN: 978-1-945967-67-2
Library of Congress Control Number: 2017907853

Second Edition: July/2017

10 9 8 7 6 5 4 3 2

ZIMBELL HOUSE PUBLISHING
UNION LAKE

Dedication

For Liam and Vaughn who made me tell Ralphy stories over and over. ~ *XXOO*

For my children, Dana, Sam, and Nick, who prompted some of the ideas, thank you, and I love you.

Contents

Ralphy Saves the Lighthouse   1

Ralphy the Giant Candy Bar   11

Ralphy Makes New Friends   19

Underpants to the Rescue   35

Apples, Pears, or Cherries?   49

I Got One! I Got One!   57

The Cat Witch   65

Glow   73

Smile!   85

Three Nuggets   95

The Winged Avenger and Four Horses   107

Chameleon Chaos   121

The Paper Boat Race   133

Slapped by a Salmon   143

Strrrriiikke!!!   157

Linda D. Vagnetti, Author

Erin Abramowicz, Illustrator

Discussion Questions

Ralphy Saves the Lighthouse

School was out for the summer, so my mom, sister DiDi, and Gramma-Nona decided to take a trip and visit the great lighthouses of Michigan. I really didn't have a choice.

Even if I had my own opinion about this or anything else, nobody cared what I thought. DiDi, however, thought it was a great idea because she was eleven years old, not to mention the fact that anything I, her little brother, didn't like, my much older, wiser sister thought was awesome. Pff. Older, sure, but wiser? I don't think so!

"There are a million things I can think of to do instead of lighthouse hopping," I mumbled to myself. "Maybe one of my friends will need a blood transfusion. I might need to help the lifeguard at the city pool. My friend Doug got a whole set of race cars last week for his birthday. Who is going to help him try them out?"

When I gave these reasons to my mom, she just stared at first and then replied, "You're going."

When you're a kid, and your parents say you're going, well, you're going. This so called adventure was supposed to start in Alpena, Michigan, and then we were to travel from lighthouse to lighthouse all around the state.

Some of the lighthouses have rooms you can stay in for the night. That part I was supposed to be really excited about. I mean, think about it. I had an absolutely great bed at home, and all my friends were there too. Gramma-Nona, however, was very excited because staying in a lighthouse seemed like a great adventure to her.

When we got to the first lighthouse, I dragged my feet and played around outside. Spotting a beehive, I started poking at it with a stick.

DiDi saw me and screamed, and Mom yelled, "Ralphy, get over here!"

I dragged my feet making lines in the dirt, and then I stepped on my shoelace and it came untied.

Finally, Gramma-Nona came back to me and used her grandma voice, "Please Ralphy, won't you do it for me?"

Geez, I thought. *Fine. I'll run in and out. Who cares about this anyway? NOT ME!*

"I don't want to go in," I said. I didn't let on, but I could see there were some cool things inside, especially in the light tower. After visiting the first one, I began to have a little more interest in the workings of lighthouses. We learned that kids actually lived in these places and didn't have to go to school in the olden days. The light room at the top of the stairs was pretty cool. I especially liked all those winding stairs. I didn't let on though that I was interested at all. *But if I could save a ship, I would be the greatest hero ever!*

My imagination took hold as my mind wandered into a scenario where nobody but me can save a thousand men on a ship. Only I can save the ship with all the life-saving food supplies for a whole city. I turn the light by hand and save the day. DiDi thumped me on the head, bringing me back to reality, and we left.

DiDi talked to me non-stop in the back seat about how cool the lighthouse was, so by the time we arrived at the second lighthouse at Whitefish Bay, she and I wanted to know everything about lighthouses and the people who lived in them.

George Patrick O'Reilly lived in this particular lighthouse. He had a full white beard, wore a sailor's cap, and smoked a pipe. I was mesmerized by him immediately. His voice was gravelly and kind of fun to listen to. When George talked, his mouth slid to one side to hold his pipe in the corner of his mouth. I couldn't figure out why the pipe didn't fall out. I thought he kind of looked like Santa Claus. Wondering if he was in fact Santa, I thought how much fun it would be to talk to him.

I made a mental note to set my alarm clock next Christmas for the middle of the night. Maybe I could catch the real Santa in my house.

Anyway, DiDi and I really did want to hear all about his lighthouse and his life.

George told us he had no family, but some lighthouses that are too far from a town have real families that live in them. He explained to DiDi and me that when lighthouses were first built, the shipping lines paid a man and his family to live in them. Any children they had were homeschooled.

"Kind of cool," I said, "but what about friends, and why do we need lighthouses?"

George gave out a hearty laugh and said he had all day to spend with us if we really wanted to know the whole story. He sat back and began to tell us all about lighthouses and their value.

"Huge ships have sailed the Great Lakes for over two-hundred years. There have always been areas where there were no cities with safe harbors or lights to guide the ships through dangerous waters or storms. Storms on the Great Lakes can be very treacherous, and without a safe place to head into, many ships would sink with everyone on board, not to mention all the precious cargo they might be carrying.

"The cargo was often oil, food, or other things people really needed. So lighthouses were built on the edge of the shore where there was no other light. If a ship was in trouble, the lighthouse's bright light would guide them through a dangerous area where there might be rocks, show them how close to land they were, or give them a place to pull in and wait out a storm."

DiDi and I were fascinated by George's story. "George, I think lighthouses are awesome, " I confided in him.

George continued telling us about the many times a lighthouse, just like the one we were in, had saved ships and all those aboard. "I was a sailor for many years, and this very lighthouse saved my ship from certain disaster during a storm. I knew at that time, I would come and live in this lighthouse when my years of sailing the Great Lakes were over, and here I am."

George stopped his story and looked outside. "Hey, there is still a little time before dark. You two want to wander around the grounds for a while?"

Outside, I saw what seemed like millions of fireflies. "Hey Mom, can I collect some fireflies in a jar?" I asked.

"No," she said. "They might get loose inside overnight."

But, as usual, I didn't really want to listen. Most of the time, I didn't think her noes were reasonable, so I got a jar, and soon it was full of fireflies. I didn't do it to be mean or anything, I was just curious about them and wanted to watch them for a while. I poked air holes in the lid and added some leaves for food. I hid the jar under the bed in the room that DiDI and I were going to sleep in that night.

I was pretty proud of myself for being able to get away with this bug jar considering Miss Know-It-All was in the same room. Every once in awhile, I got them out and watched them for a bit and thought, *How are they going to get out? It's not like they know how to unscrew the lid.*

We had a great dinner, played Monopoly for a while, and then went to bed. We had been sleeping for a little while when I suddenly woke up to a booming sound. I sat straight up in bed and saw huge flashes of light through the small window in our room. I dashed to the sitting room and found George in there too.

"Hey, Ralphy," George said, "Looks like we're in for quite a storm."

I felt my curiosity rise and eagerly asked, "Can I stay up and help with the light?"

"Sure, I am just about to fire her up," he said. I had to ask him why he said her instead of him. George explained that most things that are helpful are usually called her. I'm not sure I agree, but it was not the time to argue with him.

Suddenly, a siren sounded and George jumped to his feet and ran to a nearby cabinet. He flung open the door and grabbed a red phone. "I'll have it lit right away," he told whoever was on the other end. "Hang tight and hold your course."

He put down the phone and ran amazingly fast up the winding stairway. I followed right on his heels, even though he was taking the steps two at a time. At the top of the stairs, we entered a large room with an enormous circular glass in the middle. All around the room, there were windows, and in the middle of it all, there was a huge light with glass doors every few feet all around it. Earlier, DiDi and I learned that this room was called the Optic or Lantern Room.

George reached for a large red switch and flipped it up. Almost immediately, a blinding light blazed from the circular glass and began spinning in a slow circle.

"There's a ship out in the storm, and it's taking on water," George said. "They're afraid the rough waters may cause the ship to break in half. They need a safe place to put in and ride out the storm."

Just after the light made its first trip around, there was a massive crashing sound, and I heard the shattering of glass. Then there was nothing but darkness, wind, and rain.

George grabbed me as he flipped on his flashlight. He slapped the flashlight against his leg, but the light coming from it was pretty dim. "Darn," he said to himself. "I forgot to replace those batteries, and I don't have any more available."

"What the heck just happened?" I asked shakily.

George yelled over the howling winds that the storm blew a large tree branch right through the

Lightroom. The limb had smashed through the glass and broken the light, leaving only darkness. "The light cannot be fixed quickly enough," he yelled. "I have to think of something, I just don't know what to do."

Then, I heard the ship's loud horn sending out another distress signal as the crew was once again in the dark, not knowing how close to the treacherous rocks they were getting. "If the ship hits those rocks, it will surely sink," I whispered.

Suddenly, I knew what to do. I grabbed the flashlight from George, darted to the stairway, and slid quickly down the banister. When I got to the bottom, I ran to our bedroom and reached under the bed. There they were, the fireflies I had captured, and they were all lighting up like crazy. I raced back up the stairway carrying the jar.

I hurried back into the Lantern Room and put my jar into the remaining mirrored parts of the enormous light. Immediately, the fireflies began to light up. Each one looked one hundred times brighter than it normally would look because of the mirrors inside the light.

George was on the red phone talking to the Captain of the ship. He was explaining to them what happened to the light. I could hear the Captain yelling that things were getting too rough out there and something had to be done soon if the ship and its crew were to be saved.

Then, George got a questioning look on his face, "Yes, yes, this is the lighthouse. You can see the light?" George looked back at me.

"Yes, yes," came the joyous reply. The Captain said he could see where he needed to take his ship.

George sat down and just looked at me for a minute. "How did you ever think of that?" George asked me. "Your idea and quick thinking probably, no, *definitely* saved that ship."

Later on, I was thanked again and again by the Captain and many of the other crewman. I was given a big hug from my mom and Gramma-Nona.

"This was one time your not listening worked out," they all laughed.

The next day, as a man fixed the light, I let my fireflies out of the jar.

"Go and tell all the other fireflies what heroes you are," I told them.

Everyone laughed, and some of the men on the ship rubbed my head. "That's for luck, and you sure were lucky for us," one said to me. "Thanks, Ralphy."

After things had quieted down a bit, DiDi said to Mom, "Boy, I bet Ralphy's in trouble this time! I heard you tell him no fireflies and—"

Mom lifted up her hand, stopping Miss Big-Mouth in mid-sentence, and said how proud she was of me, and that she should be too. DiDi's face fell, and she huffed away the way girls do when they lose.

This time, for once, I was not grounded. However, it would be kind of cool to be grounded in a room here in this amazing lighthouse. I couldn't wait to tell my friends back home about George and his story.

Ralphy the Giant Candy Bar

"Please Mom, it's the best field trip of the year. You have to let me go. I'll listen, I swear I will. Pleeeaaase?!"

I was trying everything, but my mom was definitely leaning toward not signing the permission slip for the field trip to the candy factory.

Usually, she went on all the trips, but this time she had to attend a fundraiser for DiDi that she had already promised to help with.

What's more important, I thought, *the candy factory or Girl Scouts selling stupid cookies at the mall? Is there even any question?* I mean, she could sell those cookies by herself or with her troop or with someone else's mother. I thought of this field trip as the chance of a lifetime. I could envision real candy being made before my very eyes. Candy is probably one of my most favorite things. I never thought I would get a chance to see it actually being made from beginning to end.

Naturally, I wanted to back up my position, so I said, "Mom, it's always about DiDi." I knew this wasn't exactly true, but I was willing to try anything. If pleading wouldn't work, maybe guilt would. I waited as Mom decided whether she'd let me go or not. I knew she didn't want to sign the permission slip because there were a couple of times I had gotten into a little trouble. *Big deal, you'd think I planned to knock people off their feet when I turned on that fire hose. Geez, it was an accident!*

"You can't seem to get ahold of your curiosity about things," she said, "and you never listen."

"That's not completely true, Mom. I start out listening. I do! It's just that sometimes my curiosity gets in the way. Now that I'm more mature, it won't happen again. I'm sure."

"Ralphy, you have to promise," Mom said reluctantly.

So I promised to listen to the teacher and any and all chaperones. This was going to be the best field trip of the year, and I would have chopped off a foot if I had to because I didn't want to miss it.

Finally, Mom gave in. "Okay, Ralphy. I'll sign your permission slip. But remember, you've promised to do your best to listen. Don't forget."

I couldn't believe my ears. "Mom, you're awesome! The best mom ever!" I shouted. I truly meant what I said this time. I planned to do everything I could to be, and stay, on my very best behavior. I told myself if I just give it a chance, I would see everything I needed to, just like everyone else in the class. It sounded perfectly reasonable at the time, and I relaxed thinking about the candy.

★★★

All the students in my second grade class were wearing matching yellow shirts with 'Potter Elementary School' printed on them. Several schools were visiting the Gummy Works Candy Factory today, and our teacher didn't want any kid mix-ups. Each school had a different color shirt. I giggled a little to myself when I started to fantasize about what would happen if we all changed shirts without the teachers knowing. Then, I snapped back to reality and mentally slapped myself for even having those thoughts.

As the bus pulled into the parking lot of the candy factory, my curiosity was beginning to fire up. *I just have to stay with everyone else and learn all about how to make candy,* I thought to myself.

Then I began to wonder how they get the chocolate on top of the candy bars.

I wondered how they got the nuts in some of the candy.

I wondered if the colors of the Bottle Caps were in tubes or bottles.

My brain just wouldn't quit wondering about everything. That is what usually gets me in trouble. But I promised to be good, so I forced myself to stay in line with the rest of my classmates. As we were shuffled along, we passed huge containers of fudge and caramel and nougat.

"Awesome," everyone was mumbling, and I started to twitch with curiosity. I tried to control my brain, but the questions kept popping in. *I wonder... I wonder...* what if this, what if that? I was going coo-coo wanting to know about everything, and to know about it—RIGHT NOW!

Then, they told us we were going to see how a candy bar was made. There was a certain area with big machines and a conveyor belt that moved slowly. We were supposed to sit in a room at the end of the conveyor belt and watch the best candy bars in the world come out. Afterward, we could each have one.

But that was not good enough for me. I couldn't stand it any longer. I had to get closer and see everything that really went into the making of a candy bar, not just sit and wait for the candy bars to come out. I needed to be a part of it. I wanted to see the inside workings of the candy room where the candy bars actually began.

I saw my chance, and I couldn't help but take it. "Mr. Turner," I said kind of frantically. "I have to use the bathroom, please." Mr. Turner was the dad who was watching my group.

He said to me, "We'll be waiting down the hallway where the candy bars come out. Just hurry so you don't miss anything."

I felt a little guilty, but what could it hurt? I thought I'd be right back even though I knew what I should be doing. I sneaked into the first door I saw. It said "Keep Out", but you know me. I couldn't control myself, so in I went.

Suddenly, *Swoosh!* I was off my feet and being tossed around like a ball. Something sweet and gooey was swirling all over me.

"Now this can't be good," I said. Suddenly, something grabbed my belt loop, and I was being carried along with a lot of other gooey pieces of candy. All I could think was, *OMG.*

"Help!" I screamed as I landed with a plop onto something white and soft. I felt so sticky and heavy that I was having a hard time moving my hands and feet. The nougat, nuts, and chocolate were holding me in place as they hardened on me. I tried to get up so I could get off the conveyor belt before reaching the viewing window, but I felt myself moving along the conveyor with other much smaller candy bars. I couldn't seem to move my arms or legs. The candy had hardened all over me, and all I could do was lay there and wait for the end of this experience, and the end of me. I thought, *It's all over now,* but then something began hitting me in the head.

Nuts! I was even being pelted with nuts, which also stuck to me, and the viewing window was looming ever closer.

Some workers saw me, and they yelled at me to get off. I yelled back to them that I was stuck, so they tried to pull me off the conveyor belt. When they tried to grab me, they couldn't get me off because I was pretty well stuck, and the conveyor belt had started to move a little faster, maybe because of the extra weight. Anyway, the workers couldn't help me, so I moved along, soon to be in full view of my whole class. As usual, I thought *what WERE you thinking?* but it was too late.

An automatic door opened, and the conveyor belt I was on entered a room with windows all around. *Oh great! Just perfect,* I thought.

There was my whole class sitting in chairs waiting for the candy bars to come out. I saw their eyes widen and pop open with surprise when this huge candy bar with my arms, legs, and head sticking out came into view.

When they finally realized it was me, the kids all started yelling. The teacher started yelling. Then, of course, I saw Mr. Turner. He had forgotten all about me until now. I saw him looking around, and I knew that he suddenly realized that I had never returned to the group. And there I was, sticking out of a giant candy bar—a great big, nosey, gooey, mess.

The conveyor belt finally stopped, and I just laid there and closed my eyes as everyone crowded around me laughing and pointing.

"What should we do now?" the kids asked my obviously surprised and embarrassed teacher.

"Well," she exclaimed with a shrug of her shoulders, "we might as well have a piece of Ralphy!"

The kids thought it was a great idea. Everyone started cutting pieces off of the giant candy bar until I was free.

Except for the goo in my hair and on my clothes, I was fine for the time being. The kids started laughing at me again, but, of course, that was after they all had some of MY candy bar. I was a bit embarrassed, but embarrassment was definitely not my biggest concern. I was okay right then, but what would happen when my mom found out?

"I don't suppose there's any chance of you not telling my mom?" I said to my teacher. Like that could even work, since thirty kids knew and couldn't wait to tell everyone they knew what happened. But it was worth a shot anyway. Maybe I could become a hermit, and no one would come over. "Or maybeee ... oh just forget it," I said. I was so busted this time.

"This has been quite a little adventure hasn't it, Ralphy?" my teacher said as she ignored my simple request.

"Uh, yeah, I guess it has been," I whispered. "I was just curious to see inside the candy bar room, and I couldn't help myself. I just had to get in there. I didn't think this was going to happen. I'm sorry." I tried to convince my teacher of my remorse, but when I really thought about it, I wondered how many people actually got to see a candy bar from the inside. "Deep inside," I said to myself. It was probably the most flavorful bit of accidental trouble ever.

"Only you, Ralphy, only you," my teacher laughed.

★★★

At first, my mom didn't find my little adventure too funny. She was pretty mad and disappointed in me. Mom being disappointed is really the worst punishment ever. I felt so bad that I didn't live up to my promise, but I didn't feel bad about the adventure. It was definitely worth it. I didn't say that part out loud, though, to anyone.

Needless to say, I am telling this story from my room, which I will see a lot of this next week. Once again, I am grounded, but this time, I'm kind of a school hero too. Everyone wants to know just how it feels to be a giant candy bar.

Ralphy Makes New Friends

"Happy. Am I happy? Happy about what? My life is at a standstill." I mumbled to myself. "Ralphy the friend, Ralphy the neighbor, gone, over, the end."

I had established myself at my school and in the neighborhood. It took years of my life, a lot of planning, and all for what? We were moving away to a new home, a new city, and a new school. No way was this my idea.

You have no say in what happens to you when you're a kid. Parents just do as they please, and you're dragged along like another piece of furniture or something. Mom said it would be an adventure.

"Well, when I want an adventure, I'll make my own," I continued mumbling as I packed. Even DiDi was upset. She just knew she'd never make another friend, not ever!!! You know how dramatic girls can be.

I was curious about the new house, but then I am pretty curious about everything. We turned onto the new street, and I said to myself, "What a stupid name. Treetop Drive, yuk!" The house didn't look too bad, but I just knew the rooms were small and smelly like kids' old socks and tennis shoes, *double YUK*, I thought. *What if I found old undies? Triple YUK. I don't see any kids either, probably because there aren't any. I bet it's a kidless area, or worse. Maybe they banned kids around here. It figures my parents would get sucked into something like that. I bet they don't even have a school here. If there is a school, it's probably full of zombie kids with bad attitudes and mean old teachers who turn into witches at night. I bet, I just bet.*

My brain just would not stop the negative and scary thoughts. I knew I'd have to really be on my guard. Time for a pep talk. Yeah, that's what I needed. So I said to myself, "Once again, my very survival might be—no, my survival *is* definitely up to me. I'll be ready for anything they throw at me. I'll show all of them. I'll pretend I can't talk, and then everyone will leave me alone. Yeah, that's what I'll do at school... if there even is a school."

When I finally forced myself to go inside the house, I was geared up to hate everything. Then something weird happened.

Hey, I thought, *this house is sort of cool.* There's a curved banister to slide down and a big fireplace too. My room was kind of okay; it wasn't too small, and my nose detected nothing foul. I slowly opened the closet and peeked in with one eye. If something or someone were in there, I'd only lose one eye. *Nothing smelly or scary in here, and it's really clean. Hmmm.*

I looked outside and saw that the backyard had a tree swing, and there were woods behind the fence. It was kind of scary looking back there, dark with huge branches reaching down everywhere. I had to shudder, but I was sure there weren't any bears back there. At least, I didn't think there were any bears.

"Hey Mom, are there bears in those woods?"

"No, Ralphy, there aren't any bears in those woods."

"Whew, I wasn't really too scared. But you can't be too careful when it comes to bears," I said to no one but myself.

★★★

On my first day at Beechmont Elementary School, my teacher turned out to be Mr. Dotson. *So much for the mean, old lady witch,* I thought. *Gee, I've never had a man teacher before. This might be kind of cool.*

There were twenty-six kids in my class, and everyone said, "Hi," or "Glad to meet you." Everyone was smiling and very friendly. Well, almost everyone.

In the back of the class sat a kid with flaming red hair. He had freckles on top of freckles, and he reminded me of a bushy haired strawberry—if strawberries had hair, that is. He was kind of big for his age and had an "I couldn't care less who's new" look on his face. He didn't even look up when the class started welcoming me.

Curious as usual, I asked the girl who sat next to me, "Who's that kid with the red hair?"

Her name was Alba, and she said, "His name is Clifford Headstrom, and he doesn't ever talk to anyone. All he does is read books. I don't think I have ever even seen his face. He is a real science geek, and no one really bothers with him."

Yikes, I thought, *if everyone here thinks like her, this adventure could end up as bad as I thought—a never-ending nightmare.*

At recess, I saw Clifford sitting by himself with his head in a book, so I walked over and said, "Hi, I'm Ralphy Seaford, and I'm new here."

"Yeah, so what?" he replied.

"What are you reading?" I asked as he flipped me a sour face and rolled his eyeballs.

"You really won't understand it, so there's no point in telling you."

"Oh yeah?" I said. "Well I'm probably just as smart as you are, and I think you're acting like a jerk. So I don't want to talk to you anyway. I just thought since you and I both like science, you might be interested in the science kits I got for Christmas. But forget it. You just sit there by yourself."

As I walked away, out of the corner of my eye, I saw him look up and watch me. I kept on going and joined some other kids who were playing wall ball, and I started to play too. It was fun, and then recess was over.

Two of the kids playing were named Paul and Wesley. They both lived a couple of blocks away from my new house. They asked me to come over, but I couldn't stop thinking about Clifford and why he didn't want to be friends. It always bothers me when I don't know the why of something. It must be genetic because my mom has to talk to everybody she meets, except that she tells everybody everything. If you are unlucky enough to be with her, a stranger might learn the last time you brushed your teeth or the first time you did potty on a real toilet. I have a lot more self-control and simply ply them with questions instead.

After school the next day, I thought I would try again. This time, I just started walking with Clifford and asked if he saw the eclipse of the Sun on the news.

At first, there was no reply, and then Clifford said, "Yeah, I saw it."

I continued to talk about how I was new and didn't know anyone. He remained mute like always.

At lunch the next day, I sat with him and ate my lunch. There wasn't much conversation, but Clifford didn't move away either.

The third day, he asked me to come over and see his science lab, and that was how we became friends.

After we had hung out for a couple of weeks, something weird happened. Clifford said he hated his name and was thinking about getting a nickname.

I laughed. "Well, we could call you Jabber."

"Well, let's see," Clifford said. "Hmmm… Jabber… you know, I think I like it."

"Dude, I was only kidding," I laughed. "'cuz when you get talking about something scientific, there is no stopping you."

"Well, I really do like it," he replied. "From now on, Jabber it is. Now that we are really friends," he said, "there is something I have to show you. You know I disappear every day for a while after dinner. Well, there is a reason for that. Meet me tonight about seven-thirty in the woods by the big oak tree."

I quickly agreed because I was definitely curious. I waited in the woods like Jabber asked. Like always, my brain began to work overtime. *What if Mom is wrong. After all, how many woods with or without bears has she been in? Do owls bite you on the neck? Why are those bushes moving so much? Maybe I should grab a big stick.* Before I could freak out and run, out of nowhere, I saw a flashing light coming toward me. This really scared me for a minute, until I realized that it was Jabber.

"Come on and follow me, Ralphy."

"Where are we going?"

"Just wait and see. It's not too far."

We walked deep into the woods and out the other side, ending up on a dirt road that stopped at a massive iron gate. Jabber climbed over the gate calling to me to jump over too. He had a large bag which he had thrown over before he climbed up and flipped over the gate. I reluctantly followed him over the gate.

Once on the other side, I saw a huge old house with dead trees all around it.

"Where are we? I'm not going near that place. It looks haunted," I said.

"Well it sort of is," Jabber laughed. "Come on scaredy cat."

We got up to the door, where Jabber knocked three times. After the first knock, my feet wanted to get going in the opposite direction. After the second knock, I got freaked out about what might be going to open that door. I had butterflies the size of turkeys running around in my stomach. *What am I thinking? I don't even know this kid,* I thought, *this is just another one of my nosey blunders.* But I told myself I had to get it together and quit imagining the worst.

After about a minute, the door began to slowly open, creaking and groaning.

My hair felt like it was standing on end, and I just wanted to run screaming into the night, but I certainly didn't want to be a chicken either, so I stayed put. The door opened completely, and there stood a kid about our age. He had curly hair that was dark and bushy. He reminded me of a big, hairy spider. Plus, he was really skinny. His clothes were hanging on him like garbage bags. I was totally convinced he was going to suddenly disappear or something equally weird.

Jabber slipped in quickly and motioned for me to follow. My feet didn't want to move, but in I went. The big door closed with a slam behind us.

Once inside, Jabber explained how Jerome Lebeanne had run away from a foster family.

"Jerome thought that he was just kind of in the way after his foster parents had a baby of their own," Jabber said. "He figured they probably didn't want him anymore, but they didn't really know what to do about it. So he ran away, broke into this house, and has been stealing food and things he needed for a few months now. One day, I came here to get some special glass that's in the windows of some of these old houses. I needed it for an experiment. When I got in and was trying to carefully remove one of the windows, I heard something. It was then I discovered Jerome. He tried to hit me with a chair, but I ducked just in time. I was pretty mad, so I chased him, got him in a headlock, and asked what in the heck he was trying to do. Jerome told me the whole story, so I've been bringing food and things to him ever since. Until you and I became friends, there was no one I trusted enough to tell about Jerome."

"Wow! Don't you go to school or anything?" I asked Jerome.

"Well no, not now," Jerome answered. "I want to though. I just don't know what to do."

I started to think about that and then said, "I have an idea. It might take a few days, but maybe I can do something."

We hung out for a while, laughing and talking about everything, from my move to Jabber's new name.

"I want a nickname too," said Jerome.

Jabber and I looked at each other, and I said, "Well it's got to be something like the bean from your name. After all, you are really skinny, like a *bean*pole. So maybe something kind of classy like a play on your last name. How about LeBean?"

"Perfect," smiled Jerome. He was happy with his new name.

I could not believe how well the three of us hit it off. Jabber talked about all the inventions he tries to make. Then LeBean told how he had been left at a church as a baby. Then, he had been in three foster homes. He had been an all 'A' student and even had a touch of magic about him. Sometimes, if he became really upset, he could move things just by thinking about them, and sometimes he saw things that might happen before they actually did.

I said "All I can do is try everything. I have lots of great ideas, and I usually—no, almost always— have a hard time controlling my curiosity." All in all, we decided we were a perfect trio of friends.

That night, we left Jerome and were on our way home when I said to Jabber, "How long have you been going there to see Jerome?"

"Only a few weeks, but he's starting to feel really lonely being there all alone all the time," answered Jabber.

I quietly thought for a while and then said, "You know, I really like him, Jabber. I may have a solution to this."

"I have, I mean, my parents have some friends who are always saying they wish they had a son. They can't have a baby because they travel a lot for work. But they really are nice people and would be great as parents."

"Do you think they would consider getting involved with just some kid who ran away from home?" Jabber asked. "They'll probably think he's a criminal or something."

"Well they can check it out, and if everything he told us is true, maybe something will work out," I answered. "We'll have to wait and see."

We secretly continued to visit LeBean for about another week. Each time we went, he was super happy to see us, almost too happy. Something had to be done fast. We played games and talked about everything. When we left, LeBean was always sad.

Then one day, something happened. LeBean didn't answer the door. When we climbed in through a window, he wasn't in the house, and neither were his things.

I knew I should have told my parents right away. They always say you should listen to your conscience. If doing something doesn't feel right, it probably isn't. Now if something has happened to LeBean, it was my fault. Once again, my not listening was ending up badly.

Jabber and I panicked, so we ran to my house and found my parents waiting along with two police officers. When we came running in, my dad told us to sit down. *This can't be good,* I thought. Jabber and I glanced quickly at each other as the questioning began.

One police officer said he had a few questions for us about a boy who has been illegally living in the old abandoned Mason place. We tried acting like we didn't know anything. This was met with a frown from my dad. The police officer said they had found out about LeBean and had taken him into custody.

"You mean, like to ... *jail?*" We said simultaneously.

Now things were getting too serious, and I knew we had to come clean about LeBean, so I took a deep breath and started to explain his situation.

"I was going to tell you, I just didn't do it soon enough," I said to my parents.

"Jabber and I had this idea. Well actually, I had the idea. I was thinking about your friends, the Crosses. You're always saying how they would be great parents and how it is too bad they travel so much. So, I thought LeBean might be the answer since he isn't a baby. He could always stay with a friend when they were both gone at the same time."

"It seems like you've been giving this a lot of thought, Ralphy," Mom said. Leave it to Mom to see the good side of anything you do. "You know, though, we've told you never to go on private property, let alone break into a house, or however you got in. But you didn't listen, and something dreadful could have happened to this boy. You guys were wrong, both of you."

"By the way, Jabber, your parents are being informed next. You're not skating out of this one," Dad added.

Jabber left and said he would tell his parents. The policeman left, and I was left to face the music. My parents said that they needed to have a serious conversation with me. This I was definitely not looking forward to. I hate that guilty feeling. My parents seem to love me having it.

After they were done lecturing me, I was once again grounded to my room for the weekend. "Maybe you'll be able to make a better decision next time," they said.

Naturally, DiDi had been eavesdropping in on the event. She had to get in her two cents worth about how I never listen. "Yeah, this is just like you, Ralphy. No common sense. Just thinking about yourself. Nosey, nosey, nosey, that's you, with no thought of the consequences. When will you grow up? I mean, really."

I answered with, "Okay, miss perfect. If you ever blow it even a little bit, I'll never let you forget it." I rolled my eyes, telling her to try minding her own business if she had any, and closed my door. I wanted to slam it, but then I'd be grounded next weekend too. It sure is an unfair world when you're young.

I kind of felt sorry about LeBean being discovered, but deep inside, I also knew it was probably for the best. We were a great trio for a while though.

Jabber called a little later in the day, and my mom let me talk to him for a few minutes.

"I got into trouble too," exclaimed Jabber. "I can't blow up anything in the yard for a week. It's like torture. I have this new compound that I was going to try on a pumpkin. I think it will just blow the seeds out if I cut off the top."

I was kind of skeptical about this one, but I was in no mood to argue, so I said, "Look, I'll help you de-seed a pumpkin next weekend. Hey Jabber, I can't talk right now. I'll call you later," I muttered.

A week passed with no news about Jerome at all.

Jabber and I didn't talk about it much, but we were both pretty quiet. Jabber even told me he didn't feel like blowing anything up. I knew the situation was getting too serious.

Then, just when I felt all was lost, something pretty spectacular happened. I came home from school, and there were three cars in our driveway.

Inside were the Crosses and two people I didn't know. They turned out to be Jerome's legal foster parents.

My parents said everyone was talking and trying to work something out for Jerome. The Crosses were willing to take him home with them for two weeks and see how things went. The problem was that the Crosses lived in another state so Jerome might not be around here if they decided to have him live with them.

"I'm just glad for LeBean that you guys are trying to work it out," I said.

I told Jabber what was going on, and he was happy and sad at the same time.

A few weeks later, LeBean showed up at my door.

My parent's yelled, "Surprise!" then the Crosses yelled, "Surprise!" and then LeBean yelled, "Surprise!"

"So what's going on?" I asked, stupefied.

The Crosses explained that it didn't really matter where they lived. They really like having Jerome, and since we were such good friends, they'd decided to buy a house here. After I had stood dumbstruck for a few minutes while this info registered, I reached for the phone, which, as usual wasn't on its base. After looking around frantically, I paged it, and we heard a muffled ringing coming from the couch. I grabbed the phone, called Jabber, and before we could count to fifty, he was running in the door to join in the celebration.

We asked if we could have a campout sleepover that night. The parents all said, "Of course." We threw a tarp over the clothesline, threw rugs on the grass, grabbed pillows and blankets, and of course, flashlights. We climbed into our makeshift tent and listened to the night sounds. The night was perfect with chirping crickets, a lone owl, and rustling branches.

Normally, any one of us would have been scared silly, but we were three, so inside the tent, with only our flashlights, we made a secret oath to always be best friends. Together, we would be the fearless trio, or maybe the *awesome trio*.

Everything was perfect until there was a crack of thunder and a flash of lighting, which sent all three of us bolting up to the house, each of us trying to get through the backdoor at the same time.

Underpants to the Rescue

Yay! School was out for the summer, and everything was just great. The awesome trio—me, Jabber, and LeBean—sang as we walked, skipped, and ran together on our way home.

"We are going to have the best summer ever," I said.

LeBean said, "I know I am. The Crosses have a cottage."

"I've been there," I told him. "But it'll be a lot more fun now!"

We couldn't wait to begin our first summer together as the awesome trio.

Our Boy Scout troop was planning a weekend of survival training on Moorhead Mountain. Moorhead is just outside of town, and it is all dirt on one side, and all wooded on the other. Our troop was to practice wilderness survival to earn a merit badge.

The only problem was that LeBean wasn't in the Boy Scouts yet. This meant the awesome trio would have to be a duo. He was going to join, but Mr. Cross had been out of town a lot the past couple of months, and in order to join, your dad had to be active in the Scouts too.

The week before the outing, the leaders were going over the rules for the weekend at the preparation meeting.

Jabber was at his grandma's birthday party, so I said I'd get all the directions down for the both of us. I was having trouble concentrating because the den leader seemed to be going on and on about nothing. I was mostly daydreaming about us surviving all odds on Moorehead Mountain, and I guess I missed one important part.

Each group of three scouts was supposed to leave a trail of something they could use to find their way back to the camp, like piled up rocks, or pieces of cloth tied to a branch.

Each group was going to go in a different direction and follow their own clues back to camp. I missed the 'follow your own clues back' part. I did, however, get the part where he told us we could bring one person if we wanted who wasn't in the troop. Since LeBean had not joined yet, this was perfect.

As I walked home, I talked to myself about how I wanted to tell LeBean and Jabber that we could all go. Oh yeah! It was going to be the three of us blazing a trail through the wilderness. I was completely geeked!

Of course, LeBean wanted to go, so Jabber and I went shopping with him to get the necessities: a canteen, a flashlight, boots, a compass, and a bug bite kit. The less needed, but more wanted, necessities were candy bars and the fake poop I bought on our last family trip. This I kept a secret from the others. LeBean already had a backpack, so he was all set.

I tried to get up early and be super quiet, but mothers have a sixth sense. It's like they're psychics or something. Just try to pull something over on them, and somehow, they always seem to know something's up. I thought I could sneak out, and then out of nowhere, she appeared at my bedroom door. She gently reminded me that I had to listen to the scout leaders, and she kissed me goodbye too many times.

At almost six o'clock on Saturday morning, we all met up at the troop leader's house. There were fifteen boys and two troop leaders. We loaded all our gear onto a bus, and we were off.

Jabber kept asking me if there is anything special we were supposed to do. I said no because I didn't think there was. Jabber was skeptical but forgot about it once we started singing songs. We sang *Row Row Row Your Boat,* and *She'll be Coming 'Round the Mountain.* Then we all sang a rousing Boy Scout version of *Living on a Prayer* by Bon Jovi. That's the one we all really liked. LeBean did a rap song about scouts on a mountain.

Everyone thought he was pretty cool.

We finally arrived at the bottom of Moorehead. The troop leader said, "Okay boys, we will have to walk from here to the campsite. Carry your supplies in your backpack. Some areas of this trail are narrow and steep, so until we get to the camp, you will all be tied together with a rope in case someone starts to fall."

The first part of the climb was not just "kind of narrow" it was barely wide enough for our feet.

"Yikes," whispered Jabber, "this is kind of scary."

"Just keep going," I said, "and try not to look down."

LeBean kept looking at me like I was coo-coo or something. Finally, I said, "WHAT?"

He said, "This is very cool. Thanks, Ralphy."

There's that guilty feeling, I thought, but I just shook it off and was glad I didn't say anything mean to him.

Everyone was pretty serious at the beginning, then as the trail widened, we began having more fun.

We reached the campsite at about noon and immediately started setting up our tents. We didn't really know how to put up a tent completely right, so when the whole thing came down on LeBean's head, we laughed until one of the leaders came to help us. We divided into groups of three, with each group making up a name for themselves. Our group was called the L.T.P.s or "Lucky Three Pals."

That night we had a raging bonfire where everybody tried to scare the bejeezus out of everybody else by telling ghost or werewolf stories. One was about a guy who liked to catch Boy Scouts and eat them for dinner.

"Are you for real? Really," I asked, and everyone laughed, but then I know we all secretly wondered if it could be true. After that, all of us brave scouts pretty much bolted into our tents.

I never thought I'd be so happy to have a zipper between me and whatever. It was like that zipper was a force field protecting us from the unknown wilds of the great outdoors.

The next morning, the troop leaders told the five groups where each group's trail started. We were to reach the end of our trail and be back to camp in time for dinner, which sounded easy enough to us.

"Piece of cake," Jabber whispered to us.

"Yeah," we both agreed.

The invincible L.T.P.s started off on our trail, which was on the wooded side of the mountain. After about an hour, Jabber asked how we were going to find our way back. "The trail is not always dirt, so we really can't follow our footprints back. There are some rocky parts and grassy parts too," he said.

"All we have to do is follow our compass north or keep the sun over our left shoulder," I told him, even though I was also feeling a bit uneasy about our situation. "We can always just follow our footprint back too," I added.

"Were you not listening?" Jabber snapped. "We can't always see our footprints, remember?"

"Uh, okay," I said. "But we do have our walkie-talkies."

"Uh, oops," LeBean stammered.

"What?" I quickly yelled.

"Well, I kind of forgot to bring the walkie-talkies," LeBean whispered while kicking the dirt around with his feet.

"WHAT!!!" Jabber was hysterical. "That's all we asked you to do!"

"I know. I know," LeBean said. "I had to go to the bathroom, and then I forgot."

"Well, I hope you didn't forget your underwear too," I laughed.

"Very funny," LeBean replied, "but I'm really sorry."

"Hope we don't need them," Jabber said under his breath.

As we continued to climb, we heard water, and around the next turn, we came across a small waterfall that fell into a pond of crystal clear water. We were sweating bullets, so we decided to go swimming.

We didn't have our bathing suits with us, so Jabber said, "Let's swim in our underwear. Who cares? Nobody's around."

Jabber and I quickly stripped down to our underwear and stood waiting for LeBean, who was changing behind a tree.

When LeBean came walking out from behind the tree, Jabber and I fell on the ground laughing.

"Where did you get that underwear?" Jabber choked out with tears rolling down his cheeks, he was laughing so hard.

"I've never seen so many bright colors in one place," I snickered. "You better not let any of the other guys see those! They'll never let you live it down."

Those were the most colorful undies ever. They had stripes all over them in blazing fluorescent colors.

"Well, I got these from the Crosses just after they adopted me, and I didn't have any other clean ones. So what, they work don't they?

"WEDGIE!!!"

At that, LeBean jumped into the pond, and we followed. It felt so good that we swam for quite a while. Much cooler, we got dressed and continued on our way.

We kept walking until we reached a dead end. In front of us was a one-hundred-foot drop straight down.

"Well this isn't good," Jabber said. "Guess we better go back unless we can quickly learn to fly."

We turned back, and pretty soon, our stomachs were making growling sounds. We stopped for a snack and a drink, talked a little, and then started heading off the way we thought we had come.

It was quite a while before we stopped again and looked around.

"I don't remember this," Jabber said. LeBean said he didn't either.

I remained mute, as I knew we were lost. The trees and the plants were different than before. I glanced at my compass and discovered it was cracked, so the needle was just spinning around. LeBean looked at his, but he had sat on it and completely smashed it.

Jabber looked for his and a big, "OOPS," came out of him. "I... um... I... uh... don't seem to have it," he said softly.

"Well that's just great," I said. "We have no compass or walkie-talkies. The next thing that'll happen is there will be a huge thunderstorm or something. Some Boy Scouts we turned out to be."

No sooner had the words left my mouth then the black clouds started rolling in. The wind started blowing like crazy. Lightning and thunder were crackling all around us.

"What are we going to do?" LeBean cried.

"We have to find shelter," I answered. "Let's look for a cave or hollow tree."

"If we find one, I hope nothing's in it already," offered Jabber.

"Don't even think about that," I sniped back. "Just come on."

The rain kept getting worse, and we started slipping and sliding in the mud.

"Could this be any worse?" LeBean shouted. "It's getting really hard to see. Hey, I found something! Look at this! It looks like there's something in these rocks." A piece had fallen out of a boulder, leaving a large cave-like hole. "This looks like a good place for us to get in out of the storm. What do you think, Ralphy?"

"Let's try it," I shouted over the rain. We crawled in and lit up our flashlights, which, through some miracle, none of us had forgotten.

"I hope there aren't any things in here," Jabber whispered nervously.

"SHUT UP!" LeBean and I both shouted at him at the same time.

"The other teams will be wondering where we are soon," I mumbled to myself.

"I wonder how the other groups found their way back?" Jabber asked. "Are you sure you didn't miss something, Ralphy?"

LeBean laughed, "In Hansel and Gretel, the children left a trail of crumbs to follow back."

"Oh yeah," I slowly said. "Now I remember. There was something about leaving a trail to follow back. Like pieces of cloth tied to a tree or broken branches. I guess I wasn't listening really well."

"Imagine that," Jabber and LeBean said at the same time.

"What do we do now, 'Mr. I Never Listen'?" Jabber asked.

"I don't know, maybe they will find us in the morning."

"We will be in trouble, though. I know that for sure," whined Jabber.

"Thanks a lot," stammered LeBean. "I sure am hungry and thirsty."

"We'll eat and drink something, goofball. We aren't lost in the desert, you know," Jabber said. "We do have food and juice boxes in our backpacks."

"Okay. Everyone just relax. We'll think of something. We always do," I stammered.

"It's starting to get pretty dark over there," LeBean said as he pointed to some huge rolling black clouds just over the horizon. "Let's get on top of a rock and see if we see anything or anyone."

We found a spot, and I climbed up. At first, I saw nothing, but then I spotted movement down on a trail below us.

"Hey!" I yelled. The only answer was a huge roar. "Oops!" I cried and covered my own big mouth. It was a bear, not rescuers. "We'd better be quiet," I told the guys.

The bear kept looking up and smelling the air, but it must have lost the scent because it eventually walked away. We started breathing again, and LeBean began to freak out I can't say I blamed him. Jabber and I were kind of on edge too.

It was going to be dark soon, and another storm was definitely brewing in the distance. Suddenly, Jabber heard someone yelling. We all started yelling back, but the wind was howling and blowing our voices in the wrong direction. There were people down there who were moving away from us.

"No way," Jabber said. "We have to get their attention."

I didn't have a lot of time, so if I ever needed my imagination to kick in, then this would definitely be the time. Then it miraculously came to me.

"I know what we can do. First, LeBean, you take off those screaming underpants and tie them to a stick like a flag. Then we'll roll a big rock down the hill. When they look up, you wave those undies in the air."

LeBean got mad and said, "Why do I have to use my underwear? We wouldn't be in this mess if you would've listened in the first place."

"Well… because you have the stupidest undies on. That's why," I shot back.

"This is not the time to go over who did what," Jabber interjected.

"Oh, really," LeBean said. "We also could have used a compass, Mr. I Remember Everything."

"Whatever!" I shouted. "Let's just shut up and do it before they're gone."

I could tell LeBean wanted to continue the argument, but he shook his head and started undoing his jeans.

"Okay, Ralphy," LeBean said quickly, and off they came. He found a long stick, stood on top of a rock, and waved the underpants for all to see. Jabber and I pushed a big rock down the hill. It took a lot of little rocks with it, which we hadn't thought about at the time. I believe it's called an avalanche. Luckily, it wasn't too big, but the rocks crashed almost too close behind the search team. They all jumped and looked up. They saw that colorful, fluorescent flag of underwear waving high above them, so they called the closest search team. We were rescued just as another storm hit the mountain.

The troop leader was relieved to see us, but he really wanted to know why we couldn't find our way back like the other teams.

"I sort of didn't listen to all the instructions, I guess," I whispered. "I'm sorry I didn't listen better."

Everyone was glad we were safe, but I was grounded again, my dad informed me, as he was called to be in one of the search parties.

My dad said, "You could have been washed right off the mountain in that storm."

"No duh," I quietly said to myself, as that remark would have resulted in multiple weeks in my room.

"Don't use that 'duh' thing with me either. It's annoying," he said, and then continued with, "that was a pretty important instruction you didn't listen to, Ralphy."

Did I say that out loud, I thought. *How did he hear me? Maybe dads have a touch of that psychic thing all moms have.*

"Yes, but my underwear saved us all," replied LeBean. This lightened the mood a bit, but the grounding was still in place. The reason behind the grounding, I was told, was that even though nothing serious happened, something bad *could have* happened and I needed to learn to listen and not go off into my imagination. How this would occur in my room, I wasn't sure, but I was in no place to argue the point.

When school started up again, there was a story in the school newsletter all about how we were saved by LeBean's underwear. At first, he was embarrassed, but by the afternoon, he felt like a real hero and proceeded to tell kids they could touch the infamous incredibly colorful underpants for a dollar.

Everybody laughed, "No way, but thanks just the same."

"Really?" I asked.

"Really?" Jabber asked.

"Hey," LeBean replied, "you have to take advantage of the popularity while you can."

Apples, Pears, or Cherries?

Jabber, LeBean, and I were going to the ice-cream store for a triple dip. That was a weekly must after doing chores. School was out, and after a hard week of play and work, we took part of our allowance and went crazy at the ice-cream store.

This time, there was a sign hanging on the wall of the ice-cream shop saying there was going to be a five hundred dollar prize awarded at the State Fair for the most unique fruit tree entry. I read it first and then called the guys over to read it. Jabber was busy with his chocolate-vanilla-pistachio triple cone, and I tried to get his attention several times.

Finally, I grabbed his collar and pointed his head at the sign. We decided this was the perfect contest for us because Jabber, who was always doing experiments in his basement laboratory, had just perfected this awesome fertilizer. It would grow anything, so we knew we could have a spectacular tree.

I said, "We could have a great apple tree."

LeBean said, "I think a pear tree is better. Apple trees are too common."

"Everyone knows a cherry tree is the ultimate fruit tree," Jabber argued. We went round and round, but nobody changed their mind.

Finally, Jabber said, "Well, I'm the scientist with the fertilizer, so I think I should decide."

"Decide all you want," I replied. "I'm growing an apple tree."

"Fine," LeBean threw in, "I'm growing a pear tree."

"Well, you're not using my fertilizer," Jabber snapped.

"Fine," I replied.

"Fine," LeBean said, and we all stomped away in different directions.

This was the first fight we'd had since we became friends after LeBean was adopted by my parent's friends, the Crosses. I felt pretty bad, but not bad enough to give in.

All summer, we avoided each other. It was torture for me, but I was not going to be the one to crack. I was growing my own apple tree.

Then one day, I had enough alone time and was sick of being mad. If I did try to play with some of the other kids, all I thought about was Jabber and LeBean, so I finally gave in and called LeBean. He said his tree was doing great and then asked about mine. We decided to make up with Jabber too, but when we got to his house, he wouldn't answer the door or see us at all.

We yelled that we were sorry, but he still didn't answer. We tried looking in the basement windows, but they had been covered up so we couldn't see if he was down there. I even tried calling him, but his mom answered the phone and said he didn't want to talk. Emails were a waste of time too, as he just didn't respond.

LeBean and I tried again a week later, but Jabber was still not coming to the door. We could hear him moving around just inside telling his mom he didn't want to talk to us. A little angry, I started to talk really loud to LeBean on the front porch.

"Hey LeBean, don't you think Jabber is a great friend? Isn't he the smartest kid ever? I wish we didn't have a fight. At least, we can hang out and have a great time. Too bad it isn't the terrific trio now."

We waited for a reply but never got one. So we both shrugged our shoulders and walked off the porch. LeBean was really feeling bad, but I was just plain mad. "He doesn't have to be such a baby," I said. "After all, none of us got our way. Sometimes people feel strongly about something. You don't just drop someone because they don't agree with you."

We walked first to LeBean's house, and he never said a word. Then I went home and up to my room. DiDi tried to get me to tell her what was going on, but I said, "talk to the hand," walked into my room, and closed the door. I knew we all messed up really bad, and I felt awful.

"What a stupid fight," I said to myself.

Finally, it was time to go back to school, and the State Fair was only a week away. My tree looked awesome, and I had managed to grow a pretty rare kind of apple.

"I mean really, how different can his tree be anyway?" I said to LeBean.

The State Fair was finally here, and my whole family was anxious to go. I had my tree, and my mom was in the berry pie contest. DiDi and two of her friends made their own peanut butter out of three kinds of nuts, which they were entering in the Anything You Can Eat contest.

LeBean's family was coming and meeting us there. Jabber's family had been brought up several times, but when my mom called, they said they didn't know about a meeting. She looked at me disgusted and walked away.

Mr. Cross was out of town, but Mrs. Cross was home and eager to come for the first time. LeBean had his tree too, and we dropped them off as soon as we got there so we could look around a bit. The fair had rides, music, and games to play. The smell of candied nuts and popcorn filled our noses and then our stomachs as we walked around buying everything that smelled good.

"I'm hungry," LeBean said, so we bought more nuts and popcorn.

The Midway was where all the games were. The prizes ranged from plastic squirt guns to giant stuffed elephants. Each game was fifty cents for three tries at a ring toss or shooting a balloon, or guessing someone's age. There were colorful flags waving all around, and you could hear the merry-go-round's calliope music throughout the fair.

I should have been having a blast. LeBean should have been having a blast too. Both of us agreed that no matter how big of a jerk we thought Jabber was, we weren't having fun without him. We decided to just go back and sit by our trees and wait for the contest to begin.

The weather for the fair was perfect. It was a sunny, slightly breezy, seventy-five-degree day. Hundreds of people had shown up for the tree contest. Who was going to win five hundred dollars, not to mention bragging rights? Seventy-three trees were entered into the competition.

I said to LeBean, "I wonder where Jabber is? If he had such a great idea for his tree, where is he now?"

No sooner did I get the words out of my mouth, and just as the judges were about to start the judging, Jabber and his family showed up.

His tree was hidden under a tarp. LeBean and I wanted to see it really badly, but we pretended not to even notice him. He rolled his tree into place, and the judging began.

The judges went from tree to tree writing comments down in a book. They whispered to each other while we all waited anxiously on the edge of our seats.

My tree got a tag put on it by the judges, and I didn't really know what to think. *Maybe I won ... or maybe my tree stinks ... maybe I did something wrong, and my tree is out completely,* I thought and began sweating. I can't believe this became such a big deal.

I didn't dare make eye contact with LeBean if his tree was still untagged, no matter what it meant. Good or bad, I didn't want to see his reaction. I was certainly not going to look Jabber's way, but I really wanted to, deep inside.

Then I saw Mona Walters get a tag on her peach tree. Someone else's tree got tagged, and they had a real palm tree with coconuts on it. This made me feel a little better because that tree was pretty cool. I doubted that it would have been eliminated.

Finally, the judges reached Jabber's tree. They asked him to uncover it now to be judged. As Jabber removed the tarp, the judges gasped and looked at each other. Everyone stared in shocked disbelief.

Jabber had the most magnificent tree anyone had ever seen. It was tall, straight, and full of huge green leaves. But the best thing about the tree was that it had cherries, apples, and pears all over it.

Everybody cheered, and the judges all declared Jabber, the winner.

LeBean and I didn't know what to say or do. We just walked over to Jabber, and the three of us hugged.

Jabber said, "We'll share the prize because it took all three of our ideas to come up with this special tree."

The awesome trio swore never to fight again without talking it out.

Jabber said, "I'll practice not being so stubborn too."

We all laughed and talked about what a crummy summer it had been without each other. The three of us sat under that tree for a long time eating our favorite fruit and enjoying our friendship.

I Got One! I Got One!

"Awesome!!!" said LeBean, "I've never been fishing before."

"I went once," Jabber added.

"My dad takes me a lot," I replied, "but I never catch anything. This time, I want to catch the biggest fish ever." This was going to be an awesome weekend.

We were getting ready for a father and son fishing trip for the weekend. The father and son team who caught the most fish would be served a fish dinner by the other two teams. There were going to be lots of activities and tons of good food.

LeBean didn't have a fishing rod, so Jabber and I decided to surprise him. We pooled our money together and bought him an amazingly cool rod and reel. He was so happy and surprised; we really didn't know what to say to him. He said he'd never had friends before us, and especially ones that would buy him a gift. It was starting to get a little emotional.

"LeBean, dude, you're our friend, and we can't have a friend that doesn't have a respectable fishing rod," I told him.

Everyone laughed, including LeBean. I was glad my comment lightened the mood.

Finally, the weekend came, and we had to leave at the crack of dawn because Lake Meekey was about three hours away. This was hard for Jabber since he usually waited for his alarm to scream him out of his bed after the fourth ring. He, of course, invented the clock that went off four times, and on the fourth ring, it screamed at him. We also needed the early start because there were tents to put up, and we had to get the campsite ready before we could start our fishing tournament.

Everybody was very excited, especially LeBean who had never had a weekend with a dad before, let alone his own dad. Even though he was adopted, it felt great to him, and he was smiling from ear to ear with excitement.

Jabber was happy, because his dad usually had to work, but this time he had made the time to spend with Jabber.

My dad and I did a lot of stuff together, but most of the time, my sister DiDi went too. Her real name is Deidre, but when I was little, I couldn't say it, so she became DiDi. But this was just a guy weekend, so DiDi was going to do girl stuff with mom. Mom kept apologizing, and I kept hanging my head and saying it was okay. Actually, it was great. For some reason, dads do really cool stuff when you get them away from the moms.

When we got to the camping area, everyone pitched in, and soon the tents were up. Since none of us had been camping or fishing very often, we rented the tents. I opened ours really slowly and carefully. You never knew what could be hiding in there. I heard of a kid who found a skeleton of a raccoon in his.

LeBean, and Jabber especially, wanted to hurry and get their lines in the water. Both of them were full of confidence about catching a bunch of big fish. This optimism showed we hadn't been fishing too many times. I mean, my Grandpa loves to fish and nap. He claims you can do both at the same time. I wondered, *How exciting can that be?*

At three o'clock that afternoon, the first annual Great Fish-A-Thon was officially underway. All six of us guys threw our fishing lines in at the same time.

You have to be very patient to fish, so things didn't start out so well. LeBean couldn't keep his line in the water. He kept thinking he felt a tug. His dad finally put a bobber on his line and told him if the bobber didn't go underwater, then there was no fish on it.

"Geez!" We all said, "Can't you sit still?"

LeBean replied that he had heard if the worm was moving the fish were more likely to bite. My dad told him every fisherman has his own strategy. So he should go for it, only go for it some place where we didn't have to watch him fidget.

Jabber had his particular spot in the front of the boat. My dad and I were in the rear of the boat, and the others were along the sides.

Everyone finally calmed down, then the action started. The first fish was caught by my dad and was about nine inches long. In our bucket it went. Then Jabber's dad caught one about ten inches long, and it went into their bucket. LeBean's dad was next, but his fish jumped right off the hook and back into the water.

Then, we waited and waited. It seemed like forever when suddenly, both LeBean's and Jabber's dad's lines had a fish hooked. They both landed their fish and put them in their own buckets. LeBean caught one, and we thought he was going to kiss it he was so proud.

Before we knew it, Jabber was struggling with something on his line. He pulled and pulled. His pole was so bent we thought it might snap in half. His dad went over to help, but just as he reached Jabber, in came his fish! He caught a huge bass, and everyone except me was pretty happy.

I hadn't even had a nibble, and in my head, I thought that wasn't fair, but not wanting to be a whiney baby, I just kept my big mouth shut.

I decided my spot on the boat was probably the problem, so I thought I'd change places. I pulled in my line, checked my worm, and then cast my line again. No sooner had my line hit the water when BAM! Something hit my line. It swam under the boat, so I had to reel in fast. This fish had to be a whopper because it felt so heavy. My line was going from left to right, then under the boat again. I kept pulling, reeling, and tugging, then reeling again.

"Come on, son," Dad yelled, "you can do it!" But it was too heavy for me, and just as it broke the top of the water, it spit out the hook, and was gone.

"No WAY!" I cried. "That was really hard, but I want the prize for the biggest fish, so I'll try again. I'm not a quitter, and I'm going to do it."

An hour went by with no luck for me, so I decided to move again. In came my fishing rod, on went a new worm, then another big cast out into the water. Again, no sooner had my worm hit the water then BAM! Another fish hit, and this time I was even more determined that this fish wasn't going to get away. I pulled with all my might. I tugged and tugged, and pulled and pulled.

Suddenly, someone screamed that they had one too. It was LeBean, he was pulling as hard as he could while yelling he needed help.

My dad and LeBean's dad ran smack into each other trying to help us. They both fell over a seat, with Mr. Cross landing in a bucket of fish. The fish spilled and were flapping all over the place. By the time they got to us, everyone had heard a yell, followed by a splash, and LeBean was not standing in his spot anymore.

Before we could figure out what had happened to LeBean, I made one last mighty tug on my line and up popped LeBean holding his rod. My line was wrapped around his. I had definitely caught the biggest and the weirdest fish of all.

LeBean was hanging onto his rod while sputtering and spitting out water. Everyone looked at LeBean, and then everyone turned and looked at me. I was as shocked as anyone. We all just stared in silence for a minute.

"What the—" Mr. Cross said.

"Yeah, what the—" everybody else said.

"Yikes," I exclaimed. "Guess I better practice casting safety, but I did get the biggest one."

We pulled LeBean back into the boat and made sure he was okay, we all started laughing until we could hardly breathe. Even LeBean had to admit it was pretty funny. He never expected to be the catch of the day. Jabber was puzzled over how this could happen as he usually was about things he doesn't understand.

We saw that our lines had gotten tangled together underneath the boat on my last cast. Then LeBean just wouldn't let go of his new fishing pole.

"I didn't want to lose my rod, it was the best gift ever. I thought I had the biggest fish on my line too," said LeBean.

At the end of the day, Jabber and his dad had two more fish than me and my dad, and one more than LeBean and his dad. It looked like my dad and I were going to have to cook our fish and LeBean's fish for them.

All three of us learned how to clean fish. YUCK. But, as we were told by our dads, this is a necessity. Every self-respecting fisherman knows how to filet his catch.

At first, Jabber asked what kind of soap you used to clean fish. After several moments of side-splitting laughter, it was explained to him that you didn't use soap.

"Yeah," I said, "maybe we could just take them in the shower with us."

"Very funny," Jabber replied, "every piece of fish I ever had didn't have any dirt or scales or skin on it. How would I know, dork?"

LeBean just kept quiet and counted his catch, as he was amazed by the whole experience.

After the scaling and beheading lesson, we fried our catch over an open fire and ate them off of small sticks just like in the olden days. I don't think they had marshmallows or Hershey bars, or even graham crackers back then, but we still had s'mores.

The weekend continued with bonfires, barbecues, and games. It was one of the best times ever, and we had a great story to share at school. It was starting to seem like the awesome trio was destined for popularity at least in the storytelling category.

True to form, Jabber spent a lot of time thinking of a way to attract fish to the worms scientifically. We told him to stop thinking so much and just enjoy the weekend. He looked at us perplexed and replied, "Thinking IS how I enjoy myself."

We all just shook our heads and ate another s'more.

The Cat Witch

"Aaaaaah!!! She's at it again!" I shouted. The kids all turned to look at me. My finger was shaking as I pointed in the air. All eyes followed my finger, and over the trees, they saw the billowing, greenish-black smoke.

"That's the smoke from the Cat Witch's house. She lives alone in the spooky old red house, the one with the rock wall all around. Whenever she catches enough cats, she makes cat stew or cat pie. She loves cat stew." I said. "I have seen cats wander over that wall and they have never... been... seen... again. I've heard howling and whimpering coming from that direction when the wind is right. So stay far away, and whatever you do, don't ever MEOW! This is the end of the Spooky Halloween Tour." I concluded with, "I am your tour guide, Ralphy."

LeBean, Jabber, and I decided to give Halloween tours. We were going to take kids to see the spooky woods where all the trees had huge knobby limbs that reached for the ground instead of the sky like normal trees. The next stop on the tour would be to take them past the haunted cornfield with the pecking, screaming, screeching, black crows. Not to mention the waving scarecrow. Since the wind broke its arm, it flopped back and forth, as if it were waving people into the cornfield, if they dared go in. We were going to tell them we have heard that people had been known to disappear after going into that cornfield, with only their clothes left behind at the scarecrow's feet.

We were going to end with the Cat Witch's story, and then each person who paid fifty cents would get a map of the houses that give out the best Halloween treats. The map was, of course, my idea.

LeBean was dressing like a ghost, and Jabber as a giant vampire. He is great at walking on stilts, and he wore a big cape over his outfit, so he looked eight feet tall. I was dressed in a tall hat and carrying a cane, so I looked like an old-timey mortician.

We put up signs at school and in stores, and for our first tour, we had forty-one kids who wanted to take the tour. Wow!

"We'll make a lot of money," LeBean said.

"I think the Cat Witch story is the clincher," added Jabber. "After that, they'll practically run home."

"Yeah," I said. "Then they'll tell all their friends, and we'll give another one. Not to change the subject, but the Cat Witch's place is pretty scary. I hear all kinds of weird noises by that rock wall. Well, anyway, see you tomorrow for the next tour guys. Oh yeah," I added as I walked away, "Jabber, you are great on those stilts, and LeBean, you are the best ghost ever. I especially love those noises you make. Ooooh, scary!"

I turned away from my friends and went home thinking about what a great feeling it is making money and having fun at the same time.

Later that night, I was in my backyard by the rock wall. The sound of whimpering came over the wall and sounded unusually loud. Smoke was billowing out of the chimney again. This time it had a purplish tint to it. Even though I'd been told a thousand times not to go onto her property, I couldn't squelch my curiosity.

"Maybe I can save this batch of cats. Maybe she has to heat up the oven before she can make the cat pie or stew." I whispered to myself. Well, I 'maybe'd' myself right over that rock wall and onto her property. I crouched down and slowly crept through the tall weeds towards those eerie sounds. As I neared a clearing, the whimpering got louder. The hair on my arms began to stand on end as I imagined what was going on.

The whimpering was getting louder, and I was sure I heard bones snapping. I began to shake all over, but my need to help those poor, defenseless animals propelled me on. I only hoped I would be there in time to save them. I worried about being turned into a toad by the witch, but I shook those thoughts from my mind and crept closer. The wind had picked up and was swirling around, blowing dirt into my mouth and eyes. The moon, which had been bright, slipped behind a cloud, making it nearly pitch black. I could hear my own heartbeat, which I knew was a good thing actually, as I slowly and cautiously continued toward the sounds.

I peeked from behind a big bush and into the clearing ahead. *Oh no, I'm too late. The old witch has already buried something,* I thought.

With my hand over my mouth, I watched as she put a rose bush in the hole, and filled in the grave with dirt. She wiped her eyes on her apron, and I heard those sounds again. Only this time, I saw that the sounds were coming from the witch herself. I saw no cats at all. Instead, the witch was planting flowers. I didn't understand, so naturally, my curiosity kicked in once again, and I had to know more.

There was a sweet smell coming from her house and flickering lights in the windows. I look all around the clearing that surrounded the house and saw a lot of rose bushes and other flowering bushes all in neat rows. The smell coming from the witch's house didn't smell like cooking cat to me at all, not that I've ever smelled a cooking cat.

Up to the old house I crept. I spied an old wooden barrel lying on its side, so I dragged it under one of the open crank-out windows and climbed up to peek into the witch's house. Expecting a gruesome sight, I half close my eyes. Slowly, I opened them and looked around. There were flickering candles everywhere. Some were in the shape of flowers, or houses, even a Cinderella style coach. There were pumpkin candles, ghost candles, and a lot of different animal candles. But my eyes nearly bugged out of their sockets when I saw what was on a shelf at the far end of the room. It was filled with different sizes of cat candles. Each one was holding a small glass with a little candle in its paws, and each one was different.

At the other end of the room, there was a big stove. On it were two huge pots of boiling liquid. In the middle of the room, the witch was bending over something on a big table. I needed to see better, so I leaned in a bit too far to see what she was doing when CRASH!!! Off the barrel I went. When the barrel fell, it broke two clay pots stacked nearby. The noise was deafening, and there was no chance of my scrambling away quickly enough now. I was tangled up in the pieces of the barrel and the broken pots. I tried to jump to my feet, but it was too late.

The witch was instantly over me, pointing her crooked finger in my face and saying in a very squeaky voice, "What are you doing by my house?"

"Uh, uh… I just wanted to see what the smoke was," I answered softly. "I'm sorry I broke your pots… I'll replace them, really. In-in-in fact, I'll g-g-go right now." I stammered as I tried to back up. I didn't know whether to be scared or sorry, or both. What I wanted was to be out of there. What had I been thinking? I'm no hero! I just knew this was going to be the last time my mom would have to worry about me not listening. I closed my eyes in case she used a vision ray to turn me into a toad. I wondered if being turned into a toad hurt. I felt sheer terror and a bit of remorse for not listening to my mom.

"Are you hurt boy?" she asked. "Would you like some hot chocolate, or how about some cookies?" When I didn't answer right away, she said, "What's your name? Where do you live?"

Geez, I thought to myself. *What a lot of questions. Maybe it's a witchy trick, but hot chocolate sure sounds good.* Once again, my curiosity took over, and I wanted to see all the candles and know more about the witch. So in I went, vowing to be super careful. After the door had closed behind me, it occurred to me that this was similar to how Hansel and Gretel got into trouble, following a witch into her own house.

After a little while of looking around and learning more about her, I thought she didn't look so scary, or like a witch anymore. In fact, she looked like a grandma.

She showed me some of the most beautiful and scary candles ever. She told me that her niece sent her big pieces of wax and different oils and dyes to make the candles with. Her niece lives pretty far away and can't visit often.

"The smoke from the chimney is from when I melt the wax in the fireplace. Then I color it with the dyes and melt it again on the stove before I form my next candle," she explained.

"So that's why the smoke is different colors," I said. "Now I get it." So I asked her about the cat candles and the rose bushes.

"Sadly," she said, "stray animals come to my door, and I take care of them as best I can. When one of them dies, I bury them and plant a rose bush in memory of the lost friend. After a while, I make a candle that looks as much like them as possible." She showed me some of the scariest and most beautiful candles ever. I was fascinated and started to feel really guilty about the Cat Witch stories.

It was time to leave, but I asked if I could bring some friends by sometime. Miss Peg—which I found out was her real name—said that she would really like that. I hadn't realized it, but there had been a metamorphosis. She had changed completely in my eyes. It's funny what your mind and stories can do. She wasn't witchy looking at all. She didn't have crooked fingers or warts on her nose. *What's safer than a grandma?* I thought.

The guys are not going to believe this one. What a surprise this has turned out to be. I told them the whole story.

At first, Jabber didn't believe me. He said, "Dude, you must have dreamed it or something."

Then they both wanted to go and see for themselves.

Miss Peg was so glad to have company; she let us each pick out a candle for our own. Although we never said so, we each felt a little bit guilty about the witch thing, so we told her we would like to do something nice for her. We offered to dig in and fix up her place a bit.

A few days later, we painted her old doors a brighter color and cut down all the tall weeds. Then we built a beautiful fence around the rose garden.

When we showed our moms the candles, they loved them. My mom took a bunch of her friends over to Miss Peg's, and they loved the candles too. With my mom's and the other ladies' encouragement, Miss Peg turned the front of her house into a small candle shop. Now, people come from all over to see and buy her wonderful candles.

The awesome trio even hand painted the sign to hang outside her new candle shop.

I have to say, we were pretty proud of ourselves. Helping Miss Peg was fun. LeBean works on the weekends at the candle shop, and I keep the weeds cut. Jabber is always inventing new scents for Miss Peg's candles.

The scariest night of my life so far, turned out to be one of the best nights ever.

The annual scary Halloween tours are better than ever, but now they end up at the candle shop, and when the kids look in the window, they see a witch stirring a big pot of who knows what?

Miss Peg loves playing along.

Glow

When LeBean, Jabber, and I went on a fishing trip with our dads a while back, we enjoyed it so much we decided to go again.

We have been friends quite a while now, and we know what a science nut Jabber can be. In his basement laboratory, Jabber, who is always inventing something, or blowing up something, invented a spray that put a fluorescent coloring on anything it touched. He made it in three colors so each of us could have our own color. He thought if we sprayed our fishing worms bright colors and made them glow, the fish would bite them for sure.

Jabber hoped the sprays would attract bigger and better fish faster.

LeBean and I think Jabber is just about the smartest kid in the whole universe.

LeBean's new adoptive family had a summer home on a lake in upper Michigan, not too far from the sand dunes. We were all going to spend a week with them on our own. We promised, well *I* promised to listen to Mrs. Cross and to follow the rules. I was so geeked because my mom said I could go at all.

"Piece of cake," I told my mom, "I love the Crosses, and I will listen to whatever they say."

We planned to fish at least three hours every day, and we all begged to try night fishing, but we didn't reveal why we wanted to go night fishing. We had sworn ourselves to secrecy about the special worm spray.

"I bet the fish won't be expecting to be caught at night," LeBean said as we each picked a different color worm spray. Jabber's was orange, mine was green, and LeBean's was purple. We couldn't wait to try the stuff out.

We got to sleep in bunk beds in one room, which meant more talking than sleeping the first night. After a pillow fight, a scary story, and talking about how to get the biggest fish in the lake into the boat, we finally fell asleep.

In the morning, LeBean's mom and dad cooked a huge breakfast, which included all of our favorite things. LeBean had his turkey bacon and apple pancakes with real maple syrup. I had a cheese, ham, and mushroom omelet. Jabber, who was always a little different, had fish sticks and potatoes with ketchup. Anyway, we were happy and full. It was time to try our luck at fishing.

We took all of our gear down to the dock to put it in the boat. The dock wasn't wide enough for all three of us at the same time, and we started bumping into each other.

Jabber, being the biggest, pretty much bulldozed his way past LeBean and me. He dumped his gear on the boat and raised his hands up like he won.

LeBean and I looked at each other, and it was like mental telepathy. We instantly knew what had to be done. We casually put our gear in the boat.

"Let's go back and get the food," LeBean said. I jumped out first, and then LeBean let Jabber climb out of the boat. LeBean climbed onto the dock and did a fake fall. As he went down, Jabber turned around to see what happened. I ran back towards them, and as I pushed on Jabber's back, LeBean grabbed his foot, and off the dock he went. Jabber fell into the water, and we were pretty proud of ourselves.

Jabber came up yelling what he was going to do to get even with us, then he started back floating and spitting water up like a whale.

"Wow," he said, "this feels great! Thanks, guys!"

LeBean and I looked at each other, and it seemed like another great idea. With a big splash, we were in the lake. We played king of the raft for hours. That's a game where you each climb on a floating raft and try to keep the others off. We were having too much fun to stop and go fishing, so I said, "Guess we'll try night fishing. How about we get those water balloons and squirt guns we brought and have a battle?"

"Yeah," Jabber and LeBean yelled at the same time.

So the first day went by in the water. I smacked Jabber right on the head with a water balloon at least ten times. My aim was perfect, and he never got out of the way in time to avoid being hit.

LeBean could hold his breath like a whale, so he kept swimming underwater and pulling one of us under by our feet.

Jabber was the squirt gun champion, hitting both LeBean and me every time. All in all, it was a great day, and no one got grounded. Usually, I ended up being grounded, but that was at my house, not here at LeBean's cottage.

After dinner and helping with the dishes, we were ready for night fishing. We packed the boat with plenty of snacks and worms. Jabber got his neon fish sprays and off we went.

LeBean's dad told us we could keep in touch with walkie-talkies if we needed to, and he and Mrs. Cross would appreciate hearing from us once every hour or so. He also told us not to be too noisy because the neighbors on the lake liked peace and quiet at night.

"Pretty BORING," we said back, "but we'll be quiet."

Mr. Cross had been letting LeBean drive the boat all summer. It was pretty easy because it was only a little fishing boat. We had our life vests on, and LeBean was doing a great job driving.

When we reached the middle of the lake, each one of us took our spot on the boat, grabbed our worm spray, and started to fish. When the worms hit the water, it was pretty cool. Each worm could be seen swimming around in bright color as the weight of the hook and sinker pulled them down.

"I know the fish are going to love these," I told them. Then BAM! Sure enough, something hit my line. I pulled and reeled until I pulled in a small bass and decided to keep it in a bucket of water. When I tossed the fish in the bucket, something happened we hadn't counted on. After a minute or so the fish started glowing green.

Then LeBean caught one and his turned fluorescent too.

We couldn't believe it. "Will they stay this way?" I asked.

"I don't know, Ralphy," Jabber answered. "I never used the stuff before either. Maybe it will wear off as they swim around."

Jabber caught three pretty good sized fish. All of them went in the bucket, glowing in beautiful neon colors. After about two hours, we had about twenty fish all swimming around in the bucket. It looked like a rainbow in there.

LeBean still had his line in when something really hit it hard. He almost lost his rod before Jabber and I could reach him to help. We all pulled and reeled for what seemed like hours.

Finally, up came a huge turtle. It was a snapping turtle which sent us screaming and scrambling to climb on the seats. The turtle was not too happy either.

LeBean yelled at us to stop moving around so much, or we'd flip the boat over.

I grabbed the gaff and prodded the turtle towards the front door of the boat.

Jabber reached down, opened the door, and I sort of shoved the turtle through the door and back into the water.

Jabber collapsed onto a seat, "I don't know how we did that, Ralphy."

We were so happy to be rid of that turtle and not rid of an arm that no one paid any attention as he swam away.

Jabber had forgotten to pull his line out of the water, and suddenly we heard his reel spinning out of control. I was the closest, so I grabbed it first and put the lock on the reel, so whatever it was couldn't get any more line out. Then I handed it over to Jabber who started reeling like crazy.

Suddenly, the line went slack, and into the boat flew a very long, bright orange snake.

"Aaah!" We all screamed.

"Cut the line over the water and get it out of here," I yelled.

LeBean reached over and cut the line as Jabber and I struggled to keep the snake over the side. *Snap!* The line broke, and the huge snake fell back into the lake.

"Let's throw in these fish and get out of here," Jabber said, "I've had enough."

"Yeah," both LeBean and I replied. We threw all the fish back into the lake.

As the fish swam away back into the lake, we all watched in disbelief with our mouths open, as there were fluorescent things swimming around everywhere.

"Oops!" Jabber said. "Maybe that wasn't such a good idea. Throwing them back I mean. I don't know how long the spray will last."

"Oh well," chuckled LeBean, "at least we are far out, and no one will notice." He started heading the boat back to the cottage.

As we got closer, we could hear sirens. "What do you suppose happened?" Jabber asked.

"I don't know," LeBean replied, "but I hope no one is hurt."

As we pulled up to the dock, LeBeans parents came running out to meet us. "Boy, are we glad you boys are back," Mr. Cross said. "We were just going to call you on the walkie-talkie. Several people have reported strange lights in the lake. The Coast Guard and the DNR are sending people to investigate. Old Mr. Tate said he saw a huge orange thing swimming under his dock. Then Mr. and Mrs. Borders called about a bunch of glowing purple things with tentacles trying to get up on their dock."

"Wow!" We all exclaimed as we looked at each other.

"We didn't see anything," I said as we went inside.

"Oh my gosh!" I whispered. "The story is growing bigger by the minute. There were no tentacles were there?"

"No," replied Jabber, "people are just panicking."

"Great experiment," LeBean adds. "We are in so much trouble when they find out."

"Well, maybe they won't find out," I told them. "Let's just be quiet and act shocked and amazed like everyone else."

Soon there were boats all over with flashing lights and nets, catching everything they could that lit up. The lake hadn't had this much excitement in years. The three of us thought the commotion was kind of cool. People were standing on their docks watching. Some were trying to get specific information from radio stations. People were talking about aliens from other planets and crazy stuff like that. Actually, it was pretty awesome.

"What should we do?" LeBean stammered.

"Well, I think we should come clean before someone gets really hurt. Grown-ups sometimes get crazy when it comes to things they don't understand, I guess," Jabber answered.

So, we decided to take the consequences and went to LeBean's dad to tell him about the spray.

"Are you kidding?" his dad said. "I'd better try to call off these guys before we owe in the thousands." He went outside and told one of the Coast Guard guys. The next thing we knew, all the boats were heading back to shore. Every once in awhile, a very pretty something would swim by. We all looked with some pride but didn't say a word.

The head of the DNR and the Coast Guard Captain pulled up to the dock and sat down to talk to us. Never before had anything struck a note of terror in me as much as the look of these guys. They had uniforms and guns. The Coast Guard guy was huge and definitely not smiling. The DNR guy sat glaring at us and looking around at all the equipment that was suddenly at hand, like trucks, boats, lights, a helicopter, and lots of men.

"Just what did you do?" they asked.

We anxiously looked at each other, and then we all looked at Mr. Cross with an appealing "please help us" look.

He was having none of it and said, "Well boys, you were asked a question."

I quickly got it that this time we were on our own. I couldn't wait until my parents got this call. "I'm toast," I whispered.

"Well sir, or sirs, I try experiments," Jabber started, "and I thought we'd catch more fish if the worms were more interesting. I sure didn't think it would seep into the fish too. Sorry for all the trouble. But I really don't know why everybody went nuts about fluorescent things in the water, it was kind of neat—" He stopped in mid-sentence as they were all looking at him like he was crazy. "I mean, sorry for the trouble I caused. Guess I wasn't thinking about what other people would think about glowing fish."

The two men listened carefully.

"Well, luckily no one was hurt, and there aren't any aliens swimming around," I offered.

"Even so, we still have to charge for our time," one of the men added.

The DNR guy wanted to know what the spray was made of. "Will it hurt the fish? Will it go away? Is it toxic to the water?"

Oops! We each thought and looked around sheepishly. Our eyes said, "Never thought about it."

"Um, we don't know exactly," Jabber admitted, "but everything I used was bought over the counter at the drugstore or grocery store. I did use some chemicals, but there wasn't a skull and crossbones on the labels of anything. So I guess the spray is relatively harmless even though kind of colorful."

The men left, saying they'd check things out tomorrow, and everybody began to calm down.

The next day, LeBean's parents made us go cottage to cottage apologizing. Some people were mad, but some thought Jabber was a genius and wanted some of the spray. Anyway, at the end of the day, we had apologized, even though we didn't see the big deal, and we were all grounded from fishing for two days.

Geez, I thought, *the Crosses must have learned from my parents ... they live for grounding.*

After thinking about it for a while, Mr. and Mrs. Cross laughingly lifted the ban on fishing. They did, however, take charge of the sprays.

The next night, there were still some very pretty things swimming in the lake, but the third day they were gone.

"Good deal, but I'm going to miss all that color," said Jabber, "But now we know there is a three-day effect from the spray. Maybe I can—" He stopped in mid-sentence as both LeBean and I jumped on him, giving him a wedgie and a noogie at the same time.

Smile!

Jabber, LeBean and I were going to the zoo with our Boy Scout troop. The guys wanted to know if I knew anything that we were supposed to do for this trip. They didn't trust me since the last time we had a troop outing.

"The underwear incident on the survival weekend was all of our faults, really. Okay, okay, I mean, it might have been mostly my fault since I'm the one who didn't get all the instructions last time," I said. "At least your underwear saved us, and I'm the one that thought of using it," I added indignantly.

The fact had been pointed out several times by Jabber and LeBean that I had not gotten all the instructions. I quickly reminded both of them that the loss of the compass and the forgotten walkie-talkies might have added to our problem.

"Ralphy, we don't want to hear it. Let's just get it right this time," they said together.

However, special instructions on how to best enjoy the animals in the zoo were given especially to US. The troop leader told US to stay in our group and not to feed the animals we weren't supposed to feed.

"There are signs posted by each animal describing both the animal and what you can and cannot do," he said.

"Got it," we all said at the same time, "GOT IT."

This zoo was pretty cool because it had areas where the animals were allowed to roam free. The animals were never in cages except when they went inside to eat or sleep. There were cement rocks around the area, then a steep wall with water at the bottom, which was usually cold and about seven feet deep. This was to keep the animals in and the people out. Our zoo is one of the only experimental cage-free zoos in the country. The animals are supposed to feel more at home we were told. Animals like gorillas, camels, lions, zebras, elephants, and a few others could spend more time outside in a more natural habitat.

The troop leader told us that everyone would be able to get excellent pictures of the animals because there were no cages or bars in the way of getting good pictures.

"But," he added while peering over his reading glasses in our direction, "we ALL have to be careful and obey the rules."

I have been fascinated by the gorillas since I was little. I have watched a lot of TV shows about them, and couldn't wait to get some great pictures of an actual gorilla for my scrapbook.

Jabber said he heard that gorillas were very smart and basically gentle animals, even though they looked and sounded pretty scary.

In his science lab, he had rebuilt a camera that was really easy to use and would take pictures quickly in a row, up to twenty at a time, like a machine gun. Once you pushed the button, you could move all around, and the camera would keep taking pictures without them getting blurry.

It was really cool, and not too heavy, so naturally, I asked Jabber if I could use it at the zoo for the gorilla pictures.

"Of course," he replied, "just be careful with it."

I was geeked about getting real close up pictures of an actual gorilla. I started wondering just how close I could get, safely that is. Then I wondered whether the gorillas like people taking their picture. I should have seen the trouble ahead when I started all that wondering. It was just like inside the candy factory before I became part of a candy bar. Thinking, wondering, and not listening are usually warnings. But, I seem to never heed warnings.

★★★

As we made our way to the gorilla exhibit, my curiosity soared. The twitching that happened at the candy factory when I couldn't control myself was coming on again. I sure didn't need a repeat scenario of the trouble I got into that time, so I tried to control it.

When we finally got near the gorilla area, a couple gorillas seemed to be having an argument. Two big gorillas were facing each other and beating on their chests. The smaller younger ones were jumping up and down screeching as they watched the confrontation.

LeBean said, "One of those looks just like you Jabber."

"Very funny," Jabber said as he pinched LeBean on the arm.

Finally, one of the big gorillas whacked the other one, and the whackee fell back, and immediately took off. The winning gorilla stood there looking proudly at the younger ones, resulting in the instantaneous stoppage of the screeching noise the younger ones had been making.

This was the gorilla I wanted a picture of. I had to get as close as possible and get the greatest pictures ever.

Both LeBean and Jabber said at the same time, "Nooo Ralphy, the Troop Leader said we had to follow the rules."

However, as usual, when I get an idea in my head, I throw caution to the wind, never even considering any possible consequences. So I leaned over and made a noise so the gorilla would look up into the camera.

Then, I decided if I just climbed out on this one big rock that was hanging over the grassy area where the big gorilla was sunning himself, I could get the best pictures EVER.

Carefully, I climbed onto the ledge. I was snapping away when suddenly I lost my balance and tumbled down into the cold water right next to the biggest gorilla ever.

Shocked, I knew I had to get out of the freezing water, so I slowly pulled myself onto the grassy area, which of course, was right next to the gorilla. I moved very slowly while keeping my head down. Then, I didn't move a muscle. I was freezing and pretty much terrified.

What was I thinking? I thought. *Apparently, I wasn't thinking, or I wouldn't be lying on the ground freezing, soaking wet next to a huge gorilla.*

Meanwhile, LeBean and Jabber were yelling for me not to move while they got help. Jabber yelled for me to take care of the camera even though it was waterproof.

Really? I thought. Then I thought, *Where's the camera?*

"Don't move or look in his eyes," Jabber said.

"Keep down and don't move," hollered LeBean. "We'll be right back with help."

The last thing I was gonna do is move and risk antagonizing this dude, I thought.

I kept my arms over my head and laid still like I was dead, which was probably going to happen for real anyway. I heard a grunting noise, and I could smell the animal coming closer. I could feel his hot breath as he sniffed every inch of me. Then he tried to gently turn me over, but I didn't move. *Can this really be happening?* Close is one thing, but this was ridiculous. *I'm too young to die!* I screamed in my head.

Then I felt something trying to grab my shirt, which was followed by a loud roar, causing me to peek through my fingers, and I saw that the gorilla that had been whacked in the confrontation earlier was back for more. He was showing a keen interest in me, but the bigger gorilla wasn't letting him get any closer to me. After that roar, the encroaching gorilla beat his chest, shook his head and moved away. After that, it was quiet for what seemed like hours.

Suddenly, I heard voices telling me that help was coming so don't panic and don't move. *Yeah like I'm going to move ... like I'm not already completely in panic mode,* I thought.

A man yelled, "We will have to clear the gorillas out of the area and get them into their building. Then we will be able to rescue you."

Always curious, I carefully looked up through my arms and saw the huge gorilla standing near me. He was looking at me and moving his head from side to side. It sounded like he was making kissing noises or something. So I raised my head a little. The gorilla stood back and started lightly beating his chest with his fists.

Fortunately, at that point, I seemed to remember Jabber saying something about gorillas doing that when they were scared, so I lowered my head again and the gorilla stopped. He moved closer and patted me on the head. Now, I was really confused about his intentions.

I raised my head up again just a little, just in time to see him reach down and pick up Jabber's camera which was lying next to me. I hadn't seen it before, but I knew this would probably be the end of the camera.

Great, I thought, *just great. If this gorilla doesn't kill me, Jabber will. Why didn't I listen? Why don't I ever listen?*

I heard a lot of commotion going on as the zookeepers were trying to round up all the gorillas and coax them into their building. All but one was cooperating. The biggest one would not leave me. He was staying close, and he had Jabber's camera.

Jabber yelled for me to not look up or move, or the gorilla would hurt me.

Easy for him to say, I thought. *He's not lying five feet from an animal that could tear him limb from limb.*

Just then, I heard another weird sound. I didn't want to look, but I just had to. I heard it again. It was a clicking sound. I heard it again and again. Finally, I couldn't stand it. I had to look. Not only did the gorilla have the camera, but he was taking pictures, pictures of me.

What the heck is going on? I thought. I could hear people laughing and cheering.

Suddenly, a hand grabbed my shoulder, one of the zookeepers was standing over me. He had Jabber's camera in his hand, and the huge gorilla had moved back. The zookeeper told me to get up slowly and follow him without looking at the gorilla.

As we cautiously slipped past, I swear the gorilla made a kissing sound. I looked sideways and realized the kissing sound was directed towards me. Then the gorilla put out his hand to me like a high-five. *This part is pretty cool*, I thought to myself. So, I slowly put out my hand, and sure enough, the gorilla high-fived me. I couldn't believe it and neither could anybody else. After we were safely out of the area, I asked the zookeeper about what had just happened with the gorilla high-fiving me and all.

The zookeeper said, "This particular gorilla is very smart. He was raised in a training school before he came to the zoo. The school had lost funding, and the study had to end. So the gorilla was sent here to the zoo to live."

When I reached my friends, I gave the camera back to Jabber. LeBean nearly choked the life out of me with his hugs, and Jabber was slapping me on the back, glad that I was okay.

Jabber looked at his camera and hit the playback button. He started laughing so hard that LeBean grabbed it from him and looked. He too began chuckling so hard that I grabbed the camera from him.

There I was, hiding under my arm on the grass. There I was, peeking through my arms, and there I was, looking very confused. The gorilla had gotten everything on film, even a shot of the people looking down at the rescue. The weirdest, but definitely most awesome part of this whole adventure was that the last picture on the camera was a selfie of the gorilla.

"Amazing," I mumbled. "Maybe I'll come back and visit him." Then I asked the zookeeper what the gorilla's name was.

"His name is Amos," he told me.

"This day has been completely awesome; no one is going to believe this at school," Jabber said. I shot a look at him, and he immediately added, "as long as you're not hurt, I mean."

I couldn't wait to tell the story at school. Jabber was glad to have his friend and his camera back, both in one piece, and I, of course, was once again grounded.

"After all the things that happen to Ralphy, why wouldn't they believe this? I really hit the jackpot when you guys became my friends," LeBean laughed.

Jabber gave LeBean a noogie and patted me on the back. Once again, the awesome trio emerged unscathed and had a great story to tell. I was just happy to be alive.

At school, we were practically heroes. LeBean even made and sold copies of some of the pictures. Naturally, he shared the money with Jabber and me. After all, I'm the one who was grounded. AGAIN.

Three Nuggets

"Yuck!"

We'd rather pull our teeth out than have a long, casual dinner at the Nugget, or any other restaurant.

Lucky for Jabber, LeBean, and me, our families all get along. Jabber and I both have older sisters, who ended up coming in handy this time around. Usually, the less we see of them, the better.

They get along pretty well with each other, except for the time they both liked the same dude. Anyway, who cares, as long as they are happy, it makes our lives awesomely easier, especially when our families took a trip out West together and the sisters came too.

We went to a resort hotel in Nevada, not far from Las Vegas, that boasted of having the best restaurant in the state. The restaurant was called the Nugget because it was located at the bottom of a mountain where the biggest gold mine in the United States had once been.

In the late 1800s, the area was a booming gold town. The Nugget Mine had been independently owned and operated by the Bellows brothers. When the mine closed, the brothers and their children kept ownership of the property and opened the Nugget restaurant. Their grandchildren now ran it. The restaurant was filled from floor to ceiling with memorabilia from back in the day. There were old picks and axes, along with lanterns and leather helmets. We didn't get the helmets because, as far as we knew, not too many guys flew into gold mines.

Anyway, they were old things, and I guess that was the point. There were pictures of real gold miners, a few of them had actually found gold, and had gotten their fortunes out of the Bellows brothers mine. The brothers, of course, received a percentage of all the gold found, making their families very rich.

"Whatever," we all said.

"Can't we just sit this one out in our room with a pizza and a movie?" Avery, Jabber's much older—as she was always telling us—thirteen-year-old sister, said she would stay with us because her social life was nonexistent way out here anyway. The parents rolled their eyes and agreed they probably would have a better time without us.

About halfway through the movie, Avery and DiDi fell asleep. The movie was supposed to be everyone's favorite, *Christmas Vacation* with Chevy Chase. However, we had all seen it about a hundred times already, so it was pretty boring. Then, my curiosity and imagination started kicking in. I couldn't stop thinking about the gold mine. What if there's still gold in there? What if the ground had shifted over the years and shaken loose some more gold? What if we could find some gold that would put all three families on easy street?

When I actually voiced my thoughts, Jabber and LeBean's imaginations started working too.

"What about the KEEP OUT, NO TRES-PASSING, DANGER, CAVE-INS POSSIBLE signs all over the place by the closed up barricaded entrance to the mine?" Jabber, who was always our pessimist, said .

"Those are probably there to keep out crowds who could cause damage," I answered.

"I think there might be some real danger involved here. I'm not sure we should do this guys," Jabber whispered.

"I would love to give the Crosses a big gold nugget," added LeBean. "They have been so nice to me. It's pretty cool being adopted."

"Well that seals the deal," I said. "Let's just go in and look around a little."

"Yeah, okay. Let's just look around," the others agreed.

Jabber, who was always prepared, as well as pessimistic, added that we might want to bring flashlights.

"You know guys, that big sign telling the story of the mining days would make a great report for my history class. I'm a little behind," LeBean said.

"Okay, let's go," I said.

Once again, the awesome trio was off on another adventure. Not listening again, and probably going to be grounded again.

When we reached the entrance, no one was around. LeBean was taking mental notes on the history of the mine. Jabber was looking around the area, and I was probing around the barricaded entrance.

"I see something sparkling inside the entrance of the cave," I said at one point. The mine was almost completely boarded up.

Jabber told us he had something to show us. "This is a jeweler's cloth from my Uncle Rod. It turns a purple color when it comes in contact with any precious metal. He uses it so he doesn't buy any fake jewelry."

That did it. Under the boards we went, and into the mine. Right away I thought I was a little unsure of this caper.

"I smell something awful; maybe there are bodies in here," whispered LeBean.

"Yeah, I smell something too, but more like sick rats or bugs," added Jagger.

"I think it just smells like old dirt, I mean how would *you* smell after one-hundred years?" I asked, trying to lighten everyone's mood.

We all laughed, relaxed a bit and started walking. At first, the ground was pretty level, and the light from the outside was enough for us to see our way, but then there was a sharp turn followed by steps leading down to another level. Just as we got off the last step, suddenly, out of nowhere, we heard a kind of *whooshing,* flapping sound. Something hit me in the head, and I screamed. Jabber grabbed his flashlight. When he turned it on and flashed it around, we saw bats. Hundreds, maybe thousands of bats. They were flying everywhere. The flashlight really set them off.

Everybody started yelling, and ducking, then suddenly, they were gone.

"We must have entered their roost," I said. "I read bats are a little protective of their homes."

"Bats give me the creeps," added LeBean. "What if they suck up all our blood, then what, huh?"

"These aren't vampire bats, and if they were, I read that they mostly like to suck on cows," Jabber told him.

"Maybe we should go back," I said.

"We have flashlights," said Jabber, "and these steps seem pretty strong."

"Let's at least talk it over," I said. Finally, we all agreed it was a go since we had come this far. Well, not all of us. I became just the teeniest bit apprehensive but went along anyway, not to be the dork.

"Oh yeah, now that it's your idea, everything is great," I snapped. I had to vent my fear a little bit, after all.

When we reached what we thought was the bottom, there was a small landing followed by another set of steps, which appeared to be much steeper than the first. The walls of the cave were getting closer, the further we went down. We could almost touch each side, and every once in awhile, a stray bat would *whoosh* by, or a rock would fall. The air was full of dust, and the smell of things rotting.

"No point in stopping now," I said, shrugging my shoulders. "I'm sure we must be near the digging area by now." In my head, I knew that this time, I may have overstepped the boundary of curiosity and entered the area of **stupidity**.

As we carefully stepped off the last of the second set of steps, we began to hear the creaking and groaning of wood. The tunnel we were in was awfully narrow, and when Jabber touched the wall, some loose dirt fell. In the dirt was something sparkling. I instantly knew we had hit the jackpot.

I ran to pick some of it up and tripped. My flashlight fell and rolled over the edge. We listened, but we never heard it hit bottom. This is when the creepies really started to get us.

"What are we thinking?" I asked.

LeBean answered quickly, though quietly, "Obviously we haven't been thinking." After that remark, we all panicked for a minute. I didn't think knees really shook, but mine were knocking together pretty good. LeBean wanted to go back and watch the movie like nothing ever happened.

"Really?" I asked, looking at LeBean.

"Okay guys, we're in a difficult spot. Let's just get out of here and pretend this never happened, okay?" Jabber said.

"Sounds like a plan to me," answered LeBean immediately.

"Oh, alright," I added, though I really didn't want to leave empty handed. It was then that I remembered the sparkling stones I had picked up, so I was ready to leave also.

Once again, nobody actually said anything, but now all three of us were more than anxious to get out of there, but it was too late. As we started to turn back, we heard, saw, and smelled trouble.

There was a loud rumbling sound above us, accompanied by a smoky smell and a cloud of dust. We looked around for somewhere to run, but we were trapped.

When I got back on my feet after dropping my flashlight, I had looked to see what I had tripped over. It was the edge of a small train track. Now, Jabber flashed his light in that direction. Sitting on the tracks, was a small mining car. Jabber shouted for all of us to get in as quick as we could. The sound was getting louder, and rocks and dirt were falling everywhere around us. There was no time to even think about another way out, I yelled to get in the car. So in we climbed, and that mining car took off like a bullet, downhill into the dark.

Down and around we flew. The car was going so fast our hair was standing on end. We went careening around and around into what??? The car was rocking side to side as the edge of the path disappeared, and we were in total darkness.

LeBean flashed his light in front of us, and we all saw it at the same time and started screaming. Someone yelled to duck just before our speeding car hit. There was a *Craaaack!* and the sound of splitting wood, followed by a very sudden stop.

Then there was light and a lot of yelling, breaking glass and crashing metal sounds all around us. We slowly peeked out of the car, dazed and confused because it looked like we were in a kitchen.

"Oh my gosh! We're dead," LeBean sighed quietly. But no, we were not that lucky, as it turned out.

"What the heck just happened, and where did you guys come from?" shouted a man with a tall white hat and clean apron.

"From the looks of the hole in the wine cellar wall, I'd say they came through there," answered another guy with a short white hat and a dirty apron.

Just then, the door to the kitchen swung open and in ran a screaming bald headed guy who turned out to be the owner of the Nugget restaurant.

For once, we were all silent, as the owner put his hands on his hips and glared at us. People from the dining room began peering through the kitchen door too. Some people had run out of the restaurant, knocking over tables as they hastily exited.

A few very tense moments passed, and then the owner began to laugh.

"You boys had a lot of guts going into that mine. I bet you had quite a ride! I was going to have that mining car brought into the restaurant, but I was told the ground was too unstable. You three are very lucky you weren't hurt crashing through that wall. My dad told me the tracks were behind there, but I never looked. Guess he was right."

Just then there was a gasp from the doorway, and three women pushed their way through the crowd, and not just any three women either.

"RALPHY!"

"Clifford Headstrom!"

"Jerome Lebeanne Cross! What in the world?"

It was our three moms, and they were in a place somewhere between worry and fury. We cringed and looked at each other, but there was no getting out of this one. Here we were sitting in a mining car with a big hole in the wall behind us in the middle of the kitchen of a restaurant.

The owner tried to explain about the car and the wine cellar wall, but this time the awesome trio, soon to be named the Troublesome Trio, was in real trouble. None of our parents wanted to hear anything.

"We just wanted to try and make us, I mean you, rich," I tried to explain.

"Yeah," Jabber added, "I even had the polishing cloth."

The parents were having none of it. This time everyone was grounded, including Avery and DiDi for falling asleep.

Later that night, we were feeling pretty blue when Jabber said, "Avery told me she's going to make all of our lives miserable when we get back home."

But that's another story. In case you were wondering, we tried polishing the shiny stones I had found. They're not gold. My dad told us they were called fool's gold and many an expectant miner had been under the same misconception that it was real gold. He then added that the saying had certainly proved to be right this time. No one said anything for once, not even me.

"Actually, it was iron sulfide with FeS_2, which gives it a brassy-yellow hue," Jabber told us later.

"Dude, like we really even care," I mumbled. "Please stop being the science guy for once."

At least this time, I was not alone in being grounded.

The Winged Avenger and Four Horses

After the awesome trio ended up grounded after our last family vacation, we were pretty surprised when we found out we were going on another.

I figured my mom was kidding when she said we were going on a vacation with five kids and three moms in the same car. Nope, she was serious, but I was glad to be with my two best friends, LeBean and Jabber. I guess it was okay if DiDi and Avery came along too. Sisters were a pain, but they usually did their own thing.

The ride was typical with a van full of kids. "Don't touch me! *Mom!* Ralphy's touching us," DiDi yelled.

"Mom, Jabber's talking with candy in his mouth," Avery complained.

"Mom, I think I'm glad I have no siblings," LeBean laughed.

"Don't make us stop this van!" two of the moms said at the same time.

We all mumbled our frustrations. This was the worst car ride ever with all the arguing and no room.

However, Mom finally said, "I'm going to STOP this van," and that ended a lot of the squabbling. It was mostly the girls starting it anyway. They are sooo picky. Sisters are a pain, but at least they usually disappeared and did their own thing when we were all forced to be together.

LeBean's parents wanted to spend some time checking out the east side of Michigan. Most of us had not been to Mackinac Island, so they decided to rent a cottage near Alpena for a week with a visit to the island for a day or overnight.

We arrived at the summer cottage early and were waiting for the dads to arrive since they were coming together after work. While we waited, we started to list all of the things we knew about Mackinac Island.

"You know, there are no cars allowed on Mackinac Island, so everyone gets around in horse-drawn carriages, or on bikes," Jabber said.

"Cool," we all said.

"We can see whose job it is to clean up horse poop if nothing else," I laughingly told Jabber and LeBean.

"Dude, that's a job?" they said together, both looking shocked and appalled.

"Hope you don't need a college degree for that one, but if you do, I mean, you'd really "clean-up" right? Joked LeBean.

"Really," I answered, rolling my eyes.

"Did you know there is a real fort on the Island?" Jabber asked.

"Cool!" LeBean and I said together.

"So if they don't allow cars, how do you get to the Island?" LeBean asked.

"By a superfast moving hydra-foil boat," DiDi said as she and Avery were walking through the room to the kitchen. They do that sometimes, just butt into our conversations. Girls, yuk.

The moms told us we were going to ride bikes around the island too and buy some of their famous fudge. You can actually watch them making the fudge. Watching was okay, but all we wanted to do was actually eat the fudge, however it was made. After all, I had seen candy really close up already, but that was another story.

Bike riding wasn't exactly grabbing us either,. I mean, you can do that anywhere, but the horses, now that was trip worthy.

Mackinac Island was about an hour and a half drive from the cabin. Then, we were going to take a hydra-foil boat across to the island. Hydra-foils are boats that ride on a cushion of air just above the water.

"How cool is this going to be?" I said to my friends. We couldn't wait.

Jabber was ridiculously excited about the hydra-foil. "I could probably make one if I tried," he said.

"Of course you can," LeBean and I said together as we rolled our eyes at each other.

Everyone helped unpack, and we had just put on our favorite cottage movie. I'm not sure who decided that it was OUR favorite, but anyway, the movie was called *Overboard,* and it's about thirty years old. We made Jiffy Pop because Jabber likes to see the bag blow up on the stove.

Suddenly, right in the middle of the movie, LeBean jumped to his feet. "Hey, what's on the wall?"

His mom got up to look at what she was sure was a knot in the paneling. That knot became the *winged avenger.*

That spot or knot was a bat. Within five seconds of the word "bat" being uttered, there were screaming people everywhere.

Some of us ran up and down the hall with the winged avenger in hot pursuit. Someone yelled to get down on the floor. That resulted in four rear-ends sticking out from under the bumper-pool table as they hid their heads. Jabber's mom was one of them.

DiDi and Avery tried to run out the double door at the same time and bounced off each other.

The bat flew down the hallway, frantically trying to get out through a bedroom window. My mom grabbed a T-shirt and tried swatting at it. Next thing we saw was my mom running back down the hall yelling with the bat flapping after her.

"Help me, Ralphy!" she squealed.

"Geez," I said, "what am I supposed to do? You're the adult!" I called back. That was probably a mistake, but it was already out of my mouth, the adult part that is. What was I thinking? I escaped her retaliation because of the chaos of the moment.

At one point, we thought we had the winged avenger cornered in the kitchen, but oh no! It swooped right past three of us and headed for the people still hiding under the pool table.

Avery stood up and tried to open the double door so it could get out, but that resulted in her trying to get back in as the bat tried to get out. The winged avenger crashed into Avery's head, and both were inside again.

The bat finally, I'm sure from pure exhaustion, settled on the wood near the corner of the family room by the ceiling. It was then that the moms decided this was a job for the dads, so we'd just wait until they arrived. Everybody was tiptoeing around so the bat wouldn't become airborne again.

When the dads arrived, things went from bad to worse. First of all, they were just as afraid of the winged avenger as we were. But with a little prodding and goading, and a little bit of begging from everybody, they decided to dress for the occasion and rid us of the creature once and for all.

Mr. Cross got some fish cleaning gloves and goggles from the closet. My dad put a deep fry basket on his head. Jabber's dad grabbed a fish net with a long handle and a ski hat with those big furry flaps to cover his ears. The pursuit of the winged avenger was on.

They chased the bat up and down the hall. The bat decided to go the other way just as Jabber's dad swung the net for the bat. When the winged avenger changed directions, my dad banged his head basket into the wall and got a pretty good sized welt over his nose. I have to say at this point, those of us who had been there all day were laughing hysterically.

Watching our fathers acting like we would if the three of us had tried to get the bat was kind of funny, then a little frightening, and then not funny at all as we were finding out that dads can be scared too. This put a whole new light on the parental protection thing we all took for granted.

I turned to Jabber, "At least we don't have to wonder when the "now you have no fear because you're a man" thing is going to kick in. Just look at them! And they're old."

"No kidding, it's kind of a relief knowing guys never grow up. I thought maybe the change would be painful," Jabber whispered back to me.

"Are you guys nuts or something? You just grow up and do your best. I read that somewhere," LeBean added.

We thought it was just about over when Jabber's dad swung the net over the bat. The winged avenger, however, was in and out of the big holes since the net was suitable to contain a bass, not a little bitty bat. It flew out of the net and into the family room where I simply opened the double door and stood aside. The winged avenger flew out, and I closed the door. I acted like that was my intention all along, but I don't think anyone really bought it.

DiDi sneered at me, "That's sooo like you, Ralphy, taking credit for something you and your little friends didn't and couldn't handle."

"You're just sorry that you and your girlfriend didn't handle it either. Plus, it wasn't my rear end sticking out from under the table," I snapped back.

Then I thought about one of the moms under the table too and I closed my mouth.

"Okay, okay," all the parents said. "The excitement is over, so you kids better get some sleep."

We all disappeared to our rooms, and soon, everyone was asleep.

The next day, we all got up early, had breakfast together, packed a few things, and loaded into two cars. We were off to Mackinac Island.

When we got to Mackinaw City, we parked in a lot and bought our tickets for the hydra-foil ride to the Island. This was pretty exciting, but LeBean was ridiculously excited. He kept asking questions about the bridge, the boat, and the horses. He was definitely the most excited of us. He wanted to sit outside on the top deck, so the three of us did just that.

"Dude!" I said, "You need to get a grip."

The ride was smooth and fast. As we went under the five-mile-long Mackinac Bridge, we were told it was almost one hundred feet deep just a little bit out from the bridge. We were also told that there were huge ships sunk all over the Great Lakes, some with real gold and other treasures still on them.

Jabber said, "Maybe I'll invent a submarine for kids that will go down that deep with robot hands on it to pick up the gold. We could come back and go scuba diving to find some of that gold. Then we could share it and be really rich."

"I think they already have subs like that," I said.

"You don't know anything. Those aren't for kids. Mine will be different," Jabber answered.

"Whatever," LeBean and I said.

We arrived at the Island and disembarked to the sounds of clopping hoofs and rolling wheels. Right away, we saw and smelled the horses and smelled the fudge. What a great place!!! There were even big wagons being pulled by horses carrying barrels and bags in the back. Everything was being moved around by horses. I guess we had thought the horse part was sort of made up or something.

Everyone wanted to go in different directions and look around, so the moms said we could split up and then meet back at the docks at twelve o'clock, have lunch, then rent bikes to go around the island together.

"OMG!!!" Jabber yelled, "We are on our own for two whole hours. Can you believe it?"

"I can," LeBean replied.

I threw in, "Let's try not to do anything memorable. Let's just go and watch the horses and get some fudge."

Now, I'm gonna stop this story right here for a minute, and ask you, the reader, to think back. *Do you remember your mom telling you over and over again to look both ways before you cross the street? I'm sure you thought, "Geez mom, alright already, I have a brain." Right? Well, I heard it so much, I was afraid to come out of my bedroom in the morning for fear of being run over by a bus in the hallway.* Anyway, the smell of fudge and the excitement of the day wiped that caution right out of our heads.

Now, back to the story.

"Yeah, Ralphy," they agreed, and all three of us ran right into the street without looking because there was a fudge shop on the other side of the street. The next thing we knew, a huge wagon being pulled by four horses was coming straight for us.

We yelled ... the driver yelled ... people all around yelled ... so we decided to run.

The driver tried to stop the horses, swerved, and the wagon rolled over, sending barrels of something rolling down the street. The barrels were big and full, so once they started rolling, they just went faster. People were scrambling to get out of the way.

I threw myself under a parked bicycle, and one barrel rolled right over the bike and me, then smashed into the side of a building. It burst open spewing dark, thick, sweet syrup everywhere. *CAN THIS REALLY BE HAPPENING?* went through my mind. It was like watching an old movie with the wild-eyed horses with flared nostrils coming right at us. Only, I knew they weren't going to disappear like in the movies.

People ran out of the buildings and became covered with the gooey stuff. As luck would have it, two of the people were my mom and LeBean's mom.

Jabber had just stood stunned in the middle of the street. He was still standing there. I was underneath the bike, and LeBean had rolled under a bench at the side of the street.

I looked up to see several barrels careening down the street toward the people getting off the boat that docked after ours. The horses broke free from the overturned wagon and were running in four different directions. The driver chased one after the other trying to make them stop.

As my head swiveled around, I saw my mom running towards me, goo and all.

"Oomyy goodness, YIKES!!!" was all I could think to say. It had only been five minutes, and there was a disaster involving the not so awesome trio.

We were reminded of this, several times, in the following fifteen minutes. The police came, followed by the medical people. Our parents, those who'd become covered with syrup and those who just witnessed the spectacle, were kind of speechless for a few minutes.

"What were you thinking?" they all said in unison.

Being the only one capable of answering, I said, "I guess we weren't. Thinking, I mean, and it was just an accident." I continued, "It could happen to anyone right?"

Even LeBean and Jabber looked at me like I was nuts.

I continued saying that I knew the damage was pretty extensive but no people or horses were injured, and then I smiled. Oops! I realized smiling was probably the stupidest move I could make, as I was told in no uncertain terms to wipe that smile off my face. I stopped smiling, and we all proceeded to say how sorry we were.

The police officers then mentioned to our parents that they might want to consider leaving the Island and visiting another time. We were lucky we weren't being charged for the damages. Even though it was an accident, we were heavily lectured, yelled at, and grounded from swimming or fishing for two days.

We were allowed to breathe, but when I said that aloud, I was met with a not too gentle palm to the forehead. By Jabber.

Our parents decided we were not going to try visiting the Island again this year. The girls whined and carried on about how boys ruin everything, while the three of us gave no opinion.

Don't you hate when parents know things like "look both ways?"

When we got back to the cottage, we all thought it best to stay out of the way for a while. We went behind the garage and laid in the long grass. We all liked to chew on grass and suck the juice out of it.

At first, there wasn't much talking. Then Jabber started with the comment, "What are the odds that we would have two adventures in the same weekend? Both involving animals?"

LeBean started to say something, and then began giggling.

I asked him what was so funny, and he replied, "Your dad with that basket on his head."

"Yeah," I said back, "those gloves and that hat were pretty funny alright."

Then Jabber threw in, "Bats and horses, I don't know if I was more afraid of having my blood sucked or getting trampled."

Anyway, we finally became ungrounded, but we didn't go back to Mackinac Island. When we got home, I wrote down the adventures to tell at school. Our stories were becoming infamous.

Chameleon Chaos

"Your mom's gonna flip out. She hates crawly things," said LeBean.

"Yeah," answered Jabber, "don't put your name in the box, Ralphy."

"I want to see what it's like to have a pet," I whispered to them, "that's all."

Our third-grade class was sending the classroom pets home with students for the summer. You put your name in a box if you're interested in taking care of a pet, and then you write down which pet you wanted. If your name was drawn, you were given ten weeks of food if you got the guinea pig, or money for bugs if you got the big Parson's chameleon.

The Parson's chameleon is the world's largest chameleon. They are the size of a rooster or an iguana. They walk on their back legs, change colors, and they can grow back their tails if they lose them. Our class was very lucky to have one, and I wanted it. Our Parson's chameleon was named Carl. I thought he was so cool. We had a rabbit and some gerbils too, but all I was interested in was Carl.

There were thirty-one kids in the class, and twelve put their names in the box. Amazingly, I got Carl, and I couldn't believe my luck. Then I found out that I was the only one who had wanted Carl. Since LeBean was in my class, he knew the results of the drawing right away and couldn't wait to tell Jabber at lunch.

Jabber started in with, "Dude, you are gonna be so busted when your mom sees it."

"I will not," I stammered back. "My dad will step in. After all, it's not like I'm bringing home a tiger or something. He has to stay in a cage, and it will be in my room. I'll just have to clean up my own stuff until school starts again, instead of counting on Mom. Simple, right, LeBean?"

LeBean said nothing, just shrugged his shoulders and shook his head.

Now, all I had to figure out was how to introduce Carl to my family. Let's see, I think I have a fairly reasonable dad, a screaming, obnoxious, and completely crazy older sister, and a creepy-crawly-

Linda D. Vagnetti

things-hating mom. The odds were not in my favor. So, I completely covered the cage with wire and a cloth, then tried to sneak Carl carefully into the house. I sprinted for the stairs, hoping to put off the begging and explaining conversation that was definitely going to take place.

Then I heard, "Ralphy? Is that you, honey?"

Mom was calling from the kitchen, so I yelled back to her, "Yes," and that I had to hurry to the bathroom. I whisked the cage up to my room. I was really beginning to wonder if the stress was worth it. I collapsed on my bed and thought about what to do. Then it came to me. *Be honest and upfront,* I thought. *Save yourself the trouble and come clean.* So down the stairs and into the kitchen I carried Carl.

As I entered the kitchen, Mom was the only one there. She took one look at Carl and let out the loudest scream I ever heard. She covered her face with a kitchen towel and asked me what in the name of blue blazes was I doing with that *THING!*

Recovering from the sound of her scream, I calmly told her the poor thing had no place to be for the summer, and after begging and pleading from my teacher, I reluctantly said I would take him. I didn't know where that exaggeration came from, but she seemed to calm down and remove the towel from in front of her eyes slowly. Carl was cringing in the corner of his cage. I'm sure he wished he had hands to put over his ears too.

Mom uncovered her eyes and backed farther away from Carl and me.

"Ralphy, I better never see that thing out of its cage. I can't believe you brought that prehistoric looking thing home. We'll talk to your dad about this. Now, take it to your room and make sure the top is on tight."

Dad came home, rolled his eyes, and nudged me on the arm. Then said to never let IT out of its home or wherever it lived. Mom wasn't exactly satisfied with this reaction, so he threw in that DiDi would be very scared of Carl, so I'd better keep him in my room at all times, or I'd spend a lot of time in there with him.

I barely got him into my room before DiDi came home from wherever, so she remained clueless. However, she entered my room without knocking, and the screams were heard around the world, I'm sure.

Okay, a family meeting was called, and I told everyone to get a grip. Carl was harmless and even liked to sit up and beg for fruit, kind of like a cute little puppy. No one bought that one, so I just said it was my responsibility to keep Carl safe for the summer, and he would stay in my room. That seemed to fix things, so I apologized for the trouble and left the room snickering quietly to myself. A pillow then bounced off the back of my head, so I guess I wasn't snickering quietly enough.

Things at home were going pretty well. The guys and I fed Carl every day, and we even took him for walks on a special lizard leash. You should have seen people looking at us. It was really cool. Also, no bullying by anybody, big or small, occurred. We were sort of celebrities anyway due to the underwear, fluorescent worm stuff, and the gorilla selfie, so the summer was going along just fine.

Carl liked me so much that I let him out onto my bed where he curled up next to me and fell asleep. DiDi never came in my room—knocking or not knocking. Mom thought if she SNUCK in, Carl wouldn't get her.

"Really?" I said. Then one day, I found her giving him a piece of banana in his cage. Then I knew everyone had come around.

In August, LeBean's parents both had to go out of town on business over a weekend. Jabber's parents had a wedding that didn't include kids, so my parents volunteered to have them both spend the weekend with us. Since Avery and DiDi were pretty much best friends too, she got to stay over as well.

Carl being there was old news, so nothing came up about Avery being scared or anything. We were going to have a big sleepover and barbecue. The weekend started out great.

On Saturday night, we were kind of bored, so Jabber came up with the idea of putting my mom's colorful quilt on the floor and putting Carl on it to see if he changed colors as he crossed over it. That sounded like a great idea, so we laid the quilt on my bedroom floor with the door closed to see what would happen. We put him on the quilt and waited. Voila! He changed to purple on the purple squares, and red on the red squares.

"Wow!" said LeBean, "I really didn't think he'd blend in like that."

"Yeah," echoed Jabber. "This is really a cool experiment."

Just then, we heard the loudest cracking sound of thunder, followed by a blinding streak of lightning, and the lights went out.

LeBean, kind of freaked, jumped up and ran out the door. Before I could do anything, we heard screaming coming from across the hall.

The next sound out of the darkness was someone running down the hall with a flashlight. It was my dad coming to tell the girls not to worry about the lights. They screamed that it wasn't the lights, but that something had run across Avery's feet and then got into DiDi's hair.

My dad looked around with the flashlight. He saw nothing and came over to my room. I had grabbed another flashlight and tried to shush Jabber and LeBean, who had opened the door. As I looked around, Carl was nowhere to be found.

We heard a loud thud and a moan coming from my parent's end of the hall, so we all ran with our flashlights. As dad reached the bathroom, his light shone on my mom. She was lying on the bathroom floor with torn toilet paper all around her with some of the paper laying on the stairs.

"Mom, are you alright?" DiDi asked. "Why did you pull all that paper off the roll?"

"I didn't. I came in here and slipped on it. It was already all over the floor." Mom replied as she slowly got up. "What are you girls screaming about? You've had the power go out before."

"Yeah," said DiDi, "but something ran across Avery's feet and then through my hair."

"It was something fast, and it had nails," added Avery.

"Ralphy," mom yelled, "where's that lizard thing?"

"Um, I'm not sure Mom. You see, we were—"

"I don't want to hear it," snapped Mom and Dad. "You guys better find that lizard and now!"

"If I may, sir," threw in Jabber, "It's a Parson's chame—"

"I don't care what it's called," said my dad. "Just find it!"

"It's too dark," I whispered to LeBean and Jabber. "How are we going to see him?"

"I heard you," said both girls. "Why don't you use all the flashlights while we lock ourselves in our room, after we completely check to make sure that thing isn't in there, that is."

"We didn't ask you. We know how to use flashlights," growled Jabber. "We were just waiting to get them, that's all."

We looked and looked, especially downstairs since we knew Carl loved to grab things, and the toilet paper was trailing down the stairs, but no luck. When a chameleon wants to hide, he can fit almost anywhere. After about an hour, Mom said to forget it until morning and just go to bed.

"I need to find him," I said. "He will be scared being out of his home all night."

Suddenly we heard my dad's voice, "Well, you nitwits should have thought of that before you let him out and then opened the door. I wonder whose idea all of that was? How about this scenario: Jabber said 'Let's see if he changes colors,' and then Ralphy said 'What a cool idea,' and then LeBean said 'Yikes, the power went out. I'll just open the door quick and see if it's out in the rest of the house.' Is that sort of how it went?" said Dad. "Goodnight and happy hunting in the morning."

The next morning, I woke up really early, so I got Jabber and LeBean up too. "Come on, guys," I said. "Let's find Carl before everyone gets up."

Jabber wasn't really into it until we both gently reminded him who had the idea in the first place. A little wrestling and wedgies will do it every time. He got up.

We quietly slipped downstairs and began searching.

We looked everywhere: under things, behind things, in things like the washing machine, and we found nothing. Then we heard my mom asking who wanted pancakes,. I guess she was up. She asked if we had any luck finding Carl, and we had to say no. Just then, we heard a loud thud.

"What the heck was that?" questioned LeBean.

"That was the morning paper," my mom answered. "The paper person likes to try to hit the front door with the toss, so we know the paper's arrived."

Mom went to get the paper, and when she opened the door, the crazy wild dog from across the street sneaked into our house. He ran toward the dining room just as we heard the piano playing. DiDi wasn't up yet, so I knew it wasn't her on the keys.

Mom had a long skinny cloth thing across the dining room table with some fancy kind of smelly candles and a vase of fresh flowers on it for decoration. Well, the cloth thing had holes in it all around the bottom, so when the dog ran under the table, his pointy tail went right into a hole and pulled on the cloth. He kept going while everything on the table went crashing to the floor.

My mom's hands flew to cover her eyes as she began yelling for someone to do something.

The three of us boys ran to the room where the piano was and caught a glimpse of Carl jumping off the piano with that dog in hot pursuit. Mom screamed to get the dog, while I ran to get a rope.

LeBean leaped for the dog, which immediately dragged him onto the piano bench. LeBean kept holding onto the dog's collar but was losing his grip fast. Jabber jumped in and grabbed the dog around the neck as I stuck the rope through the collar.

We captured the dog and threw him out the front door, but we lost sight of Carl. Then, we heard a thunderous, "What is going on down there? What was that crashing sound?"

Then thump, thump, thump, and my dad was lying at the base of the stairs, with one sock and one shoe on, he was on his back grasping the railing. He had lost his footing and slipped down the last four steps. Luckily, he was saved by the railing.

I was speechless, and both Jabber and LeBean felt the hammer was going to come down really hard, so they both sat motionless on the couch.

DiDi and Avery heard all the commotion and were standing at the top of the stairs, hands on hips, and both had very disgusted looks on their faces.

Mom ran to Dad asking if he was alright, and Dad had this weird look on his face.

"What?" She asked.

"Well," he answered still lying there. "Carl was running up the stairs, and I grabbed for him. I'm pretty sure I killed him. As I grabbed his tail, it came off. I was trying to find out what all the noise was, and he appeared there. I guess we'll have to try to buy the class another one, right Ralphy?"

For a few of the longest minutes of my life, nobody said anything. Then Jabber, of course, chimed in. "Mr. Seaford, uh, chameleons lose their tails as a way of protecting themselves from predators. Their tails grow back eventually."

"Who cares," Mom countered. "Look at the mess here, and your dad could have been seriously hurt. I could have been hurt last night. This is pure chaos, as with every idea you guys have. Who ever heard of a lizard running with toilet paper in his mouth anyway? And while we're at it, you'd better visit those so called neighbors across the street and tell them to keep that dog of theirs in the yard and on a leash! I can't take much more!"

Dad slowly got up and looked at us on the couch. "You boys clean up this mess and then find that lizard or whatever he is. Put it in his cage, then come back down here. Girls, say nothing, get dressed, ignore the boys, and then help your mom with something, *any*thing. I'll take care of the dog."

I shot a look to Jabber to not open his mouth, then the three of us disappeared upstairs to look for Carl, who was now tailless and had to be hiding someplace upstairs.

We each took a room and began our search. I blocked the stairs with a chair and took my room. I looked around, spotting something between my dresser and the wall. On further investigation, there he was, cringing in the corner. I got him and placed him in his cage, turned on his heat lamp, and covered his cage with the wire and a cloth.

We had a very quiet breakfast. Nobody placed a special order, we just ate the pancakes my mom supplied. After breakfast, Jabber, LeBean, and I decided to clean the garage and cut the grass. LeBean said he had to go to Miss Peg's to cut her grass, but I quickly told him he was going to stay and face the music like the rest of us when his parents arrived.

We stayed as far away from my parents as possible all day, then Mr. and Mrs. Cross came over, followed shortly by Jabber's parents. They asked if everything had gone okay. Nobody said a word, we just looked at my dad.

"We just had the usual chameleon chaos," he said.

The Paper Boat Race

One day on my way home from a trip to the drug store for my mom, I spied a sign hanging outside of the park entrance. When I read it, I knew it was perfect for LeBean, Jabber, and me. It read:

PAPER BOAT RACE
TO BE HELD ON THE RIVER!

FIRST PRIZE: A BRAND NEW
DUNE BUGGY FOR FOUR

TO ENTER:

- **You must build your own boat out of paper and cardboard.**

- No power sources allowed, such as batteries or engines.

- Boat must stay afloat and move at least 1,000 feet.

- Boat may be painted.

- At least one occupant must be in the boat from start to finish.

- Sign up now with a $15.00 registration fee.

Entries will be taken at the Library from 9:00 a.m. - 6:00 p.m. Saturday and Sunday, June 18th and 19th. The race is to be held on Saturday, July 8th.

I couldn't wait to tell Jabber and LeBean. LeBean had talked about wanting a dune buggy for his cottage up north. The cottage was really close to the dunes of Lake Michigan. This could be our big chance. Once we won the dune buggy, his parents would surely let us all try it, especially if Mr. Cross was driving. *The sandy wind in our faces,* I thought, *AAAhhh, I can't wait!* I was sure we could win once the three of us set our minds to it. We are, after all, the awesome trio, are we not?

I called a meeting at my house after dinner that evening. Excitement was bursting out of my ears. I hurriedly explained the contest, and we all began to think.

Jabber, as usual, closed his eyes tightly, as his brain struggled to develop an idea. "What kind of paper or cardboard can we use?" he asked.

LeBean's face lit up. "My neighbor delivers chicken to the supermarkets around here. They are packed in very sturdy wax-coated boxes to guard against leakage. What do you think?" he suggested.

"PERFECTO," Jabber and I replied at the same time.

"Now, for a power source," Jabber said.

"We could use oars, and two of us could row," LeBean said.

"Yeah, we could, but I think I have a scientific approach to this that will make our winning a sure thing," answered Jabber.

"Really?" I argued. "This can't be something that explodes or anything like that. I don't need to be grounded again, Jabber!!! Sometimes your scientific ideas are real close to lethal disasters, you know? Remember the glow worms?"

"Yeah, did you have to bring that up? It won't be this time though," Jabber snapped back at me.

"Okay, okay you guys, what is your idea?" interrupted LeBean.

"Rubber band power," exclaimed Jabber.

"What?!" I asked. "A little rubber band to power a boat? Are you kidding?"

"No, we can make several huge rubber bands, and then attach them to big cardboard propellers. We'll use each one to propel us forward when another boat closes in," answered Jabber.

LeBean and I just looked at each other with questioning faces. "But where are we going to get giant rubber bands?" LeBean said.

"We don't get them, guys ... we make them. I have the formula for liquid rubber. All we need is a mold, and we've got giant rubber bands. I've got it all in my head," said Jabber, tapping his temple.

"Yeah, but sometimes he's a pinhead," LeBean whispered to me and laughed.

Jabber entered another world mentally, as he continued with the planning while explaining everything to us. Once again, I am the idea guy, Jabber, the experimenter is designing the boat, and LeBean is going to carry the plan through by driving the boat because he weighs the least.

Suddenly, we were all into the rubber band boat idea of Jabber's, and it even seemed feasible.

We made the rubber bands in Jabber's garage since he had all the chemicals we needed. The mold for the rubber band was a bit of a problem. Then I thought of a possible solution.

"Hey, I know, why don't we use my old swimming pool? My mom doesn't get rid of anything that reminds her of when we were little. I don't get it, but whatever."

"That's it!" Jabber exclaimed. "A pool will work great." The pool was about five feet across and about two feet deep. The hard part came next. We searched and searched until finally, we found another pool just a little bit smaller. This one was perfect to put inside the larger pool so the liquid rubber would stay in a tight circle until it hardened. That way, when the rubber was ready, it would not have to be cut into bands.

Jabber was afraid of cutting too much or too little if he had to make the bands by hand. The other pool made just the perfect size huge rubber bands.

We poured in the liquid rubber after weighing down the little pool with sand. It stayed flat inside the bigger pool so the rubber could harden.

The three of us worked on the boat for two weeks in my garage. The chicken boxes turned out to be a very good idea because they had a wax coating on them to prevent any icky, sticky, chicky juices from escaping. We painted the boxes purple and green like the Batmobile, only we named it the Batmo*boat*.

LeBean would sit in the middle of three of the boxes, which were taped and glued together. He had two chicken box cardboard oars, which stuck out of a hole next to his seat. He would use them to steer the boat, one way or the other. One oar was a little longer than the other. That way, if one became unusable due to wetness, the other would take its place. We all thought the whole idea was nothing but pure genius. The rest of the time, the oars would be raised up out of the water on the sides of the boat.

Jabber attached three double strength cardboard hooks strategically behind LeBean's seat. On the outside of the boat, directly behind each hook, was a double-strength cardboard propeller. A hole had been punched just above each propeller onto which a huge rubber band had been twisted very tightly and then stretched through the holes and onto the hooks behind LeBean's seat. After questioning how the rubber bands worked exactly, Jabber said, "Just trust me okay?"

The paint job was great, and we were very proud of our entry, *The Batmoboat.*

Finally, it was race day, the weather was perfect too; no wind and plenty of sun. People were lined up along the river with cameras, blankets, and basket lunches. This paper boat race was a really big deal. Twenty-three boats had entered the contest, and they looked like a rainbow of ingenuity.

One boat was red with ten sets of oars. Another was bright yellow with a paper sail—oh, did I mention the fact that there was no wind? Then there was a blinding fluorescent pink one. There was an orange and blue striped one, and one even that had fins to keep it afloat. Naturally, all the entries thought they were a shoo-in to win.

When the starting pistol went off, and the race began, each team was to push their boat into the water and hope for the best. It was about a thousand feet across the river to the sandy beach on the other side where the race was to end.

A silence came over the crowd as the drivers climbed carefully into their boats, hoping for the win. LeBean was a little nervous, but a last-minute pep talk from Jabber and me calmed him down. He knew just what he had to do and when.

BANG! The starter pistol went off, and the teams pushed their entries into the river. At first, everyone looked like they were neck and neck. A few boats started to sink almost immediately,. LeBean was using the oars as sparingly as possible. He pulled off the first rubber band, and the *Batmoboat* surged ahead of all the others.

Some of the boat drivers had neglected to think about steering and were crashing into each other. A couple of the boats were beginning to float off-course sideways, instead of going straight across. Five or six boats were close together, right behind LeBean.

The boat that was catching up was the boat with the ten sets of oars. It was one of the girls' boats, so all you could hear from the sidelines were screaming girls.

When LeBean tells everyone the story, this is one of the first sticking points, the screaming girls. "Why do they scream so much? I don't get it. They scream at bad things, and then they scream at good things. I had a hard time tuning them out and concentrating on going straight across.

"Suddenly, I realized that my feet were getting wet. When I looked down, I saw the water was slowly coming in through the bottom of the boxes. I knew that we were a little more than half way across, and she—the girl's boat— was coming up fast, soooo what to do?

"I decided to grab the rubber band farthest from me and let it go. The propeller kicked in and, once again, I was in the lead. Only this time, the boat was being propelled to the right. Luckily, the longer oar held out long enough for me to straighten the boat out then it bent in half.

"The last rubber band, the one in the middle, was directly behind me. Water began coming in more, and I knew it was now or never. The last rubber band was a little larger than the others, and the propeller was a little bigger too. The girl's boat was right next to me, she was using her last set of oars.

"We were about fifty feet from the finish line when I heard Jabber's voice over the screaming girls, or maybe it was just in my head. Whatever, I grabbed the last rubber band. The last and biggest propeller not only sent our boat quickly ahead, but I cut the other boat off and glided right up onto the sandy bank. It was really something! Yeah, wow!"

At the time of the win, for a minute, LeBean just sat looking around. Then it sunk in that the awesome trio was the VERY proud owners of a brand new dune buggy.

He jumped out of the *Batmoboat* and started doing cartwheels. Jabber and I both swam across the river as fast as we could.

When we reached LeBean, we all went crazy. We hugged, we rolled in the sand, and we gave each other high fives until our hands hurt. It was another one of the BEST TIMES EVER!!!

LeBean was so proud, but not as proud as we were of him. We were and still are the awesome trio. The screaming girls had become mute, but the onlookers were cheering all the more. It was an important moment to remember.

LeBean's dad had brought their boat down from the cottage, just in case we won. Now he sped across the river with my parents, and Jabber's parents aboard. Everyone was so happy and surprised. Everyone except Jabber.

He didn't get why everyone was so surprised, "Why wouldn't it work? Of course, it worked. It was simple science," he said, baffled.

Slapped by a Salmon

LeBean had been so happy living with the Crosses. Since he had been adopted, his life was becoming what he used to only dream about. He had two of the best friends anyone could have, and he was very thankful.

However, from past experience, he listened in whenever the adults around him talked on the phone behind closed doors.

LeBean knew he shouldn't eavesdrop on his new father's conversation, but in the past, secret conversations had concerned him. One example was a conversation he heard that went like this: "Well, he just isn't working out. Maybe he would be happier somewhere else." That had been followed by him being moved to yet another foster family. This time though, he heard excitement in his dad's voice, and the words "salmon", "barbecue", and "contest."

He quickly pulled his ear away from the door, feeling sort of bad about listening in, but he really had wanted to know what his dad was talking about, hoping it wasn't about him.

"Wow," he laughed to himself. "I'm getting as nosey as Ralphy," LeBean told me later, and I chose to ignore it.

At breakfast the next morning, LeBean's dad immediately began talking about the call he had gotten.

"Every year," he told LeBean, "we have a salmon barbecue at the cottage. The river down the road has rapids with a small waterfall at one point. The salmon spawn in a pool by there, and a bunch of us guys spend all day fishing for the biggest salmon. Then we all get together and have a huge barbecue. The caught salmon are kept on ice for the day, then cooked later that evening. Talk about fresh. Why, it's the best ever!"

Mr. Cross being so excited to share the story with LeBean made him feel like a real member of a family. LeBean thought about how he could make the day even better for the Crosses.

"I know, I'll tell the guys," LeBean said to himself. "Ralphy always has ideas." Sometimes, in the past couple of years, some of Ralphy's "big ideas" hadn't worked out so well, but some of them had.

He called Jabber and me asking us to come over and have a brain picking meeting.

"What's a brain picking meeting, anyway?" Jabber asked, but we both chose to ignore that.

We met at the park around the block from my house, and then LeBean told us all about the event.

"I couldn't wait to pick your brains," said LeBean.

Jabber snorted and laughed as he told us he got the "brain picking" thing now.

"Ralphy," LeBean continued, "can you think of a way we can catch big fish without waiting all day?" He turned to Jabber, "Jabber, you think about it too."

LeBean wanted to impress his new family with our fishing knowledge since we had blundered in that area twice before.

"I mean, that neon worm thing was crazy. Fun... but crazy. I sure didn't enjoy being caught by you, Ralphy, even with my new pole. Maybe this time we can succeed at the fishing thing."

A couple of days later, Jabber called all excited about an idea. We all sat in my backyard. After Jabber had told us his idea, both LeBean and I were speechless, which was a first for me.

"Really?" I replied, while LeBean said nothing.

"What?" asked Jabber, completely clueless, "What's wrong?"

"That seems kind of scary to me," I said. "Being suspended over the rapids with a net and a bag for fish. I'm not real sure about this one, Jabber."

He told us the plan one more time from the start, and we both shrugged and said, "Well, okay."

A couple weeks later, everyone was up at the cottage and the fishing day was beautiful. LeBean told his dad the three of us were going a little ways downstream to try our luck. His dad was so into the day's fishing activities, he didn't pay a whole lot of attention to what we were saying. My dad and Jabber's dad were busy with their fishing gear.

We said, "See ya later," and were off to implement our plan.

When we reached a certain spot, we had to split up. LeBean and I went across the bridge to the wooded side of the river, while Jabber stayed on the campground side.

The river was pretty narrow at this point, and we could see each other across the water. Just as the river water started to really churn, Jabber shouted for us to stop and hide behind a tree.

"Why do we have to hide?" I shouted across to Jabber.

Then I saw him reach for an arrow, and I quickly disappeared behind the tree. He grabbed an arrow and tied a rope to it, which he shot across the river to us. When we came out of hiding, Jabber said for one of us to get the end of the rope, climb up the biggest tree around, and wrap the rope around a sturdy limb.

Next, we ran the rope through a metal bracket that had a pulley wheel with a flat attachment on each side. Each end of the bracket had a flat part with two holes. We put the rope through one hole, around the wheel, then through the other hole. The pulley system was then attached to the tree with nails.

After it had been attached, one of us had to get the rope back across the river to Jabber. We didn't have a bow on our side, so we decided to throw it like a spear.

"Well, I'll try it," I said, and I did a great job even if I do say so myself.

Jabber got the rope and yelled for us to run back to the bridge and come to him.

After we had tied up the line with the pulley system, LeBean and I ran back across the bridge to where Jabber waited.

"I don't know about this," LeBean said to me. "Hanging over a swirling river only feet away from a rocky waterfall, small or big, doesn't seem like the smartest idea to me."

"Jabber is a science genius," I retorted. "He has our weight calculated along with the drop we'll need to be just over the water. If this works, we'll have the freshest salmon of anyone. Plus, we won't have to wait for hours. They will just jump into our nets. It's pure genius."

"I think we're pure idiots," LeBean said under his breath.

"What?" I questioned.

"Oh, nothing," answered LeBean. "Let's get this thing going."

I don't think LeBean was as sure about the genius part as I was, but when we reached Jabber, LeBean became excited enough for both of us.

Jabber had tied up his end of the line and attached it to the pulleys. Then he tied it in a special Boy Scout knot, and it was ready for a tryout.

The idea was to send one guy out over the river sitting in a noodle pool chair. The line could be pulled on by the person in the chair, and the chair would move along the line over the river toward the other side.

Then, the next guy would attach his chair to the line and pull himself into position. The last guy would pull the line and his chair until all three were evenly spaced across the river. Each of us had a large net and a bag attached to our chair to put the fish in. The bag should hang just in the water to keep the fish alive and fresh.

The idea was to catch the fish in our nets as they jumped upstream, then take and give all the fresh salmon to our parents. I was to be in the first chair, so Jabber hooked my chair to the line with two clamps. I climbed into the chair with my gear and started pulling on the rope over my head. My chair began to swing out over the river, and I kept pulling until I was in position. I waited for LeBean's chair.

He climbed in and pulled himself out over the river too. His face was priceless, so I reached into my pocket, took out my waterproof camera, and got a shot. He looked like he was at the end of his rope, so to speak! Then I thought, *hey how about a selfie?* So I took that one too. I didn't look all that calm either.

Things were going great until LeBean stopped himself and his chair continued sliding until it bumped into mine. We started swinging and banging and sliding around.

Jabber saw what was happening and yelled for LeBean to pull himself back a bit. My chair then started sliding into LeBean's. At least we were laughing instead of thinking of impending doom.

"Guys," Jabber yelled, "where are the clothes pins I gave you?"

"Oh yeah," I replied. "They're in my pocket." I gave two to LeBean and explained how we were to put them over the rope to the left and right sides of our chairs after we were in position. Once again, I had been too excited to really listen to all the instructions, and once again, LeBean was in the bathroom at the time instructions were being given.

We very carefully pulled in opposite directions until we were hanging about fifteen feet apart. We put our clothes pins in place, and it worked like a charm. Our chairs stayed put for the moment.

The Adventures of Ralphy and the Awesome Trio

Next, Jabber hooked up, and after he had pulled himself out over the river, I was astonished. We were evenly spread out, just like he said, and we were hanging about one foot over the water just like he said we would. However, I was closer to the wooded side, which I didn't think much about at the beginning of this adventure. It turned out that this positioning was not the best idea for me.

Even LeBean had to admit, we were pretty comfortable, dry, and no fishhooks or tangled lines were involved.

The water was rushing just under our feet. There were large rocks in front of us, then the river took a nosedive down of about twenty feet, churning and moving very fast. We could see the fish jumping around us. It was pretty cool.

At first, we made our chairs swing back and forth, having fun just goofing around. Then *smack!* A fish jumped right into my net. Jabber and LeBean got a big laugh because an especially large salmon jumped right into my chair. It slapped me pretty hard right in the face with its tail, then flipped back into the water before I could grab my net.

"Stop playing around," LeBean cautioned,. "What if we fall in?"

"Our chairs will keep us afloat. It's not like this is Niagara Falls," I said. "Relax. What can really happen? We're over about five feet of water, sitting in two noodles."

The wind picked up a bit, giving us a few tense moments as we waited to see if the line would hold and our chairs would work as life-saving devices if the line broke. The line held, and we swayed in the breeze.

"I don't know why you two guys have such little faith in me," Jabber muttered. "I know what I'm doing."

Suddenly, the fish started really jumping at us. It seemed like we were constantly catching one in our nets.

"This is great!" I shouted to Jabber.

"Yeah, I like catching better than being caught!" LeBean laughed.

Catching the salmon in the net was a little bit trickier than we had first thought. Number one, they hit the nets pretty hard, and sometimes, they were too big to fit in. But after a while, we became fairly good at snagging the fish and dumping them into our bags.

Just when I thought I had enough fish and was going to tell Jabber we should pull ourselves in, I looked over at LeBean, and his eyes were as big as Frisbees. He was pointing at me and stammering something I couldn't understand.

"What?" I shouted. Then I saw Jabber looking past me too with horror on his face. I turned around, and I realized what he was pointing at.

Seems we had forgotten one of our nature lessons about animals in the wild. The part about how there are other salmon lovers that use the rivers.

This is why we were told not to go too far from the campground or the cottage.

This is why we should have just followed everybody else. And this is why I am spending a lot of time in my room. I don't listen!

Now I'm going to meet my greatest fear and get eaten by a bear! *Aaaaaahhhh!*

The other salmon fishers were big, hairy, hungry bears. Two of which were in the water and headed straight for, you guessed it, *ME!*

I tried to pull myself across to the safe side, but LeBean had grabbed the rope and was frantically pulling the wrong way, and I joined him.

Jabber started screaming, "You're going the wrong way!"

I realized before LeBean did and stopped pulling. I yelled to LeBean, and he looked up, stopped pulling and screaming, and he saw his mistake.

However, now I was close enough to the bear to see his tonsils and his beady, hungry eyes. I reached into my bag, grabbed a salmon, and threw it right at the bear. He caught it with his very long, and probably sharp claws, then he stopped moving. I never thought I wanted to look at the butt of a bear, but I sure did then.

Meanwhile, both Jabber and LeBean had started pulling the rope toward the other side. Something was wrong, though, as I didn't seem to be moving away. The rope was stuck, and the bear, once again was coming toward me, and this time, his mouth was very wide open.

I grabbed another fish and heaved it at the bear. He missed this one, stood up on his hind legs and let out the loudest roar I've ever heard. I threw another one, and the bear caught it with its mouth. It growled with the fish in its jaws, and I really don't think he was saying thanks. Suddenly, I started to move quickly across the river.

When I looked, I saw my dad, Jabber's dad, and LeBean's dad pulling the rope. My mind bounced between being glad and terrified, as I slid along to safety.

Once on dry land again, it took a few minutes for anyone to say anything. I knew if it had been Mom, I would have been hugged, yelled at, and sent to my room until I grew up.

Dads are different though.

I got playfully whacked on the back of my head, then the words, "What are we going to tell your Mom?" came out of all three dads' mouths at the same time. I never realized how much power our moms actually had until that moment.

My dad cut the rope, grabbed the chairs, removed the hardware we had attached to the tree, then looked at us with that "what were you thinking" parent look.

I wasn't sure who was more afraid, us or our dads. It was almost comical, but laughing would be a HUGE mistake. Even I knew that.

LeBean's dad was the first one to actually break down and grab his son.

"Do you know how lucky you guys are?" he said.

Then the other two dads joined in the hugging, and I saw tears in my dad's eyes and in Jabber's dad's too.

Geez, did I feel bad or what. Then it dawned on me, all the reasons why the dads were so upset. First off, they had to rescue our butts, but now they had to face the moms, who, by the way, had sort of been responsible for our rescue.

Seems my mom asked where we were, then LeBean's mom asked where we were, then Jabber's mom demanded to know where we were. Our dads stammered on about having so much to do, and us being old enough to fish alone, but it meant nothing to our ever protective, slightly psychic mothers.

My quick-thinking dad, who remained the calmest, said he knew the spot we liked and that he'd go check on us. The other dads said they had forgotten that part and would go too.

Now, what to do was the question on all of our minds. To tell, or not to tell? That was the question. Should we spare our moms the horror of what happened, or tell all and risk the dads being sent to their rooms? Hmmm, what to do?

There was a long silence, then LeBean's dad said he thought since everything turned out okay, we could just go back, show the fish we still had, and forget the whole thing.

My dad said okay. Since this obviously was a well thought out plan by a scientific mind, and it didn't really involve not listening, he would go along just this once.

Jabber's dad sat silent and then told Jabber he would go along with the decision, but that Jabber had better develop a cold that had him staying in his room for a few days. We all got it, but for once, it wasn't me in the room. However, I sure wasn't going to say that part out loud.

We had managed to save twelve pretty large salmon and were just about to start back when we heard a rustling noise, then a low growling in the trees between us and the river. No one said a word, we all grabbed and ran. I never knew adults could move that fast. But LeBean was like a bullet, passing us all, holding his net and sprinting ahead.

When we reached our moms, Dad said, "We were racing, and boy can LeBean run fast!"

"Hey," I yelled to everyone around, "look at what we caught!"

Then, like I was hit with a hammer, I remembered we had no fishing gear on us except the nets and bags of fish.

"These fish are so heavy; we'll have to go back to our secret place to get our rods," I improvised.

The other men came in one by one, and there were a lot of salmon. We roasted corn on the grill along with zucchini. The fish was seasoned and then cooked on the grill. Some were in aluminum foil with spices, and some were on the grill whole and salted. We had potato salad, watermelon, and we roasted marshmallows until it was dark.

The next morning, LeBean and Jabber showed up at my room really early, saying they needed to talk to me. Since we were all going home that day, Jabber had started coughing like he had a cold.

"So, what's so important?" I whispered.

Jabber began by saying he wasn't comfortable with not telling our moms what had happened. "It's not like we did it on purpose," he explained.

"Yeah, and my mom is too nice to lie to. I couldn't sleep all night," LeBean said.

"Well," I replied, "I'm glad you guys feel the same way I do. I guess our dads are just going to have to face the music, but really, it was their quick thinking that saved the day."

When everyone got up, we secretly informed the dads of our joint decision. At first, we sensed some resistance, but then my dad said he was proud that lying to our moms had bothered us.

We had a huge breakfast, and when we were all seated, I started telling the story of what had happened after I had been slapped by a salmon.

Jabber's mom thought the idea was pure genius. My mom reserved judgment since I was almost eaten, and LeBean's mom looked accusingly at Mr. Cross , then said she was proud of us.

I lightened the mood by adding, "Guilt gets kids every time."

Strrrriiikke!!!

I love baseball, Jabber loves baseball, and LeBean loves baseball. What happened this year in the Astros vs. Giants championship playoffs was nothing short of the most awesome event ever!!!

The three of us all got on the Astros baseball team this year. I am pretty accurate at throwing a ball, so I played first base and shortstop. Jabber can hit a ball out of the park a lot and has throwing power, so he played centerfield. LeBean is the fastest kid on the team and can steal bases better than everybody. He is great at bunting, so he was the catcher. It seems sitting back on his haunches is a natural position for LeBean, plus he was ball fearless. The coach had said over and over "How are you going to catch a ball if you're ducking?" LeBean was the only kid who really understood this concept, therefore he was the catcher.

The season started out pretty terrible, with our team losing two in a row. Then, we began to start playing like a team instead of each guy for himself. This was when things started to improve. We were able to win three in a row. Actually, we barely eeked out the third, but hey, a win is a win.

In one game, Jabber stopped a winning home run by catching a fly ball while sliding on his stomach with his mitt behind his back. No one could believe it, especially the batter.

Talking about it later, Jabber said he had calculated where the ball would come down and where his mitt should be.

LeBean and I both said, "Whatever, dude." Jabber was clueless as to what we meant since it made perfect sense to him. He was always figuring stuff out rather than just being amazed.

At the end of the season, we were in second place, and the Giants, the nemesis of every team in the league, were in first place. The playoff game was about one week away when the kids on our team began to panic.

At first, some of our teammates were nervous and afraid to play, since some of the Giants' players had been kind of terrorizing kids on our team at the park and on the streets. Bullies are always braver in numbers, so the Giants teammates kind of ran in packs, like wolves.

When they came up to some of us, they would say things trying to get us to fight. None of us wanted any part of tangling with them. I repeatedly pointed out to our guys that we could just wait and beat them on the field. Gang mentality is stupid to me. Scary and stupid.

Jabber and LeBean, being fearless as you have probably guessed by now, revved everybody up by saying it was just a game and that we had beat them once already and could do it again.

The Giants had used different types of intimidation like signs, flags, and even cheerleaders at previous games. Seems one team always has rather frightening parents. Those were the Giants parents. They were like wild-eyed terrorists every game. They yelled at their own kids. It was kind of embarrassing. I was glad my parents sat pretty much mute, although my mom was getting a little feisty herself, especially when accompanied by Mrs. Cross.

None of the other teams liked playing the Giants either, so it became our mission to put them into their place. By the time LeBean and Jabber were finished with the pep talks, the whole team acted like they were on super vitamins or something. We were ready to play like we never played before.

Our coach's name was Frank, and his son was Pat. Pat was the team's pitcher, and although he was great, we had no other pitcher on the team. Coach always wanted Pat to pitch. He had brought us through a lot of last minute wins, and we were pretty happy with him.

When the day came for the playoff game, the weather was good, but all the players on our team were kind of nervous. There was no vomiting that I knew of, and our parents were excited and pumped us up about the fact that we could win this game too.

Parents add another whole element of stress to little league, we learned. Between screaming moms and dads, name calling to the umps, and of course, the ever shouted, 'he was safe' and 'what are you, blind?', we pretty much had to just tune them out until the game was over.

Once, a parent on the other team kept yelling that I couldn't hit, and to take my head off with the next pitch. My mom at one point leaped to her feet to go after the screamers. My dad grabbed her by the shirt and pulled her back down. We thought we were going to see a mom fight, but cooler heads prevailed, and we ended up winning that game after all.

The umpires always reminded everyone that it was LITTLE LEAGUE, not the majors, and could they please just chill out a bit in the stands. It was a lot of stress on us kids, I can tell you.

When the Giants showed up, we were all stunned. They had a banner that stretched across the entire Giants bleachers section saying, "We are #1 - The CHAMPIONS!!!" They even had their cheerleaders carrying flags that said "Champs" and all the parents wore "Champs" T-shirts. Someone had a recording of the song, *We Are the Champions,* which they kept playing until the game started. It was very annoying.

We all sat watching this spectacle, and my mom was again fighting mad, only this time, Mrs. Cross and Jabber's usually very passive mom were right in there with her. Our coach did manage to make us realize that ignoring the scene was probably the best reaction.

Our team was all nerves the first few innings, then we began to settle down and play our game. LeBean made an awesome play at home when a runner tried to slide under his tag. LeBean jumped in front of the bag, snagged the ball, and got the player before he reached the bag. We scored a run on an overthrown ball, and then they scored one on a lone home run.

In the sixth inning, the Giants jumped ahead four to one, and we started to feel a bit down. Then, in the seventh inning, Jabber hit a homerun with two guys on base, tying it up. That sparked us again, and the eighth inning stayed tied.

In the top of the ninth, we had two guys on base. After two outs, we scored one more run, giving us a one-run lead.

It was now the bottom of the ninth inning, and we just had to hold on to our lead. The silence in the stands was kind of creepy. When the Giants came up to bat, our pitcher walked three guys in a row, loading the bases with no outs.

The Giants stands were going crazy, cheering and waving their flags. Pat looked around, and we could see the sweat beads on his face. He started to wind up, dropped his head, called a timeout, and began talking to his dad.

Then, he walked over to our bench, threw down his mitt, and sat with his face in his hands. No one knew what to do, and the ump yelled that we had to resume play. Coach walked over to us and said we didn't have a pitcher, and that Pat didn't feel like he could pitch anymore.

For a minute, everyone just looked at each other, and then I heard my mom yelling, "Come on, you can do it!" and then the rest of our spectators started cheering us on too.

I still don't know what I was thinking. Something came over me—like I should take this as a 'once in a lifetime' chance to do something about the mess we were in. Before I knew it, I had jumped off the bench and told the coach to put me in.

He hesitated, as I had never pitched before, but then, neither had anyone else, so he handed me the ball. Then there was complete silence in the crowd as I stepped up on the mound. Even the Giants fans were quiet for once, at first, anyway.

The first batter stepped up to the plate. I wound up and threw. *"Strriikke,"* said the ump. The next two throws saw the batter swinging and missing. He was out number one. The next batter was the leadoff batter, who was big and hit the ball almost every time he came up to bat. I didn't care.

This was the biggest challenge ever, so I wound up and threw. LeBean caught it as the big guy swung and missed. Now, I was really pumped, the next pitch was low and over. Again, swish and *"SSSTTRIIKKE TWO"* was called.

The batter, visibly rattled, pounded the plate and raised his bat. LeBean signaled a fastball right over the plate. I trusted his instincts, and over the plate it went, making a splatting sound as it entered LeBean's mitt, and the big guy went down as out number two.

I couldn't hear or see anything but LeBean's mitt in front of me, and it looked gigantic. As the third batter approached the plate, the Giants bench and fans became silent they couldn't believe what they were seeing. My team and our fans were pretty stunned too, only they were happy.

Then, I caught a glimpse of that stupid banner saying, "We are #1" out of the corner of my eye, and threw the ball. The batter spun around as he swung, and once again that ball found LeBean's mitt. The next two pitches I don't even remember, but I heard, *"YYYOU'RRE OUT!"* and the crowd going nuts.

For a minute, no one moved as I kept my head down, walked over to that stupid banner, ran through it, and then walked back to my teammates who were now rushing onto the field and jumping all over me.

We had won the first place trophy, and if I never pitched again, and I haven't, it was the best experience of my whole life, especially when I saw the faces of my friends, family, and the other guys on the team. I was very proud and very happy.

After the hoopla of beating the Giants was over at the ballfield and the Giants had all vanished in their cars, we celebrated even more. Coach and all our fans went for triple-dip ice-cream. When Pat started to apologize for not being able to finish, we all told him not to think about it again, as he had brought us all the way to the playoffs, and the meaning of the word TEAM was helping each other.

At home, my parents told me how proud of me they were. Even DiDi said the whole thing was just too awesome, which was very high praise coming from her.

Jabber, LeBean, and I went over and over that game for days. When we saw some of the Giants around the neighborhood, they were mute.

We were learning that you can do anything if your heart is in it.

Linda D. Vagnetti. Author

Linda D. Vagnetti is a para-professional who has worked with at risk elementary students for over twenty-five years.

She lives with her husband in Michigan, has three children, Dana, Sam, and Nick, and three grandchildren, Liam, Vaughn, and Vivian.

Linda is currenty working on three children's books, along with a novel about lifes changes.

Erin Abramowicz

Erin Abramowicz is a professional illustrator, working for publishing companies and as a freelance illustrator. In December 2016, Erin graduated Magna Cum Laude from Eastern Michigan University with a Bachelor of Fine Arts degree and enthusiastically applies the foundational skills she was taught in formal education to her drawings.

She is an accomplished children's-book illustrator, having completed six children's books. Erin enjoys illustrating children's books due to her background in cartooning; growing up she was fascinated by television shows and wanted to create characters and stories like those she watched on television. Erin is eager to illustrate comic books, and has an ever-growing portfolio of work which reflects her interest in comic books, graphic novels, and animation.

In addition, Erin has designed and illustrated logos and welcomes commissions for individual works of art. While most comfortable working with Adobe Photoshop to create digital paintings, Erin also enjoys chalk pastel, oil pastel, watercolor, colored pencil, and graphite.

Erin's future, personal goals include writing and illustrating a children's book, three comic books, and creating a 2D, platformer video game. Her personal interests include nature, music, superheroes, fantasy, and ancient life.

Discussion Questions

The Adventures of
Ralphy

and the Awesome Trio

Let's Go! ASTROS

Linda D. Vagnetti
Illustrated by Erin Abramowicz

1. When reading The Adventures of Ralphy and the Awesome Trio, what was your favorite story, and why?

2. Who is your favorite character, Ralphy, Jabber, or LeBean? Why?

3. In the story, *Slapped by a Salmon*, do you agree with the boys finally telling the moms? Would you have kept quiet?

4. Are you like Ralphy in that you find it hard to listen to instructions?

5. Are you like Jabber, interested in how things work, doing experiments and "science-y" stuff?

6. Are you like LeBean, bravely willing to try new things?

7. Have you ever had to move to a new school and make new friends? Could you relate to what Ralphy went through in the story, *Ralphy Makes New Friends*?

8. In the story, *Winged Avenger and Four Horses*, a) do you think it was fair for the Mackinac Island Police to ask the families to leave the Island? Support your answer.

   b) How would you have handled getting the "winged avenger" out of the cabin?

9. In the story, *The Cat Witch*, what do you think is the moral? Have you ever been in a situation where you misjudged someone and they turned out to be a friend? Discuss the situation.

73804397R00100

Made in the USA
Columbia, SC
22 July 2017